The Dennis Wheatley Library of the Occult
Volume 27

Marie Corelli, whose real name was Mary
MacKay, was born in 1855. Educated privately
by a governess, she showed a great talent for
music, particularly the piano, and planned a
musical career. However, somewhat against
her parent's wishes, she became a writer
instead.
Her first book, *A Romance of Two Worlds*,
made little impact but *Barabbas*, published in
1894, was a real success. This was followed
by *The Sorrows of Satan* which made her the
most popular novelist of her time in Britain.
The last years before her death in 1924 were
spent in quiet retirement in Stratford upon
Avon.

The Dennis Wheatley Library of the Occult

THE MIGHTY ATOM

MARIE CORELLI

SPHERE BOOKS LIMITED
30/32 Gray's Inn Road, London WC1X 8JL

First published in Great Britain by
Hutchinson & Co Ltd 1896
Published by Sphere Books 1975
Introduction copyright © Dennis Wheatley 1975

Set in Monotype Plantin

Printed in Great Britain by
C. Nicholls & Company Ltd
The Philips Park Press, Manchester

ISBN 0 7221 2544 5

TO
THOSE SELF-STYLED 'PROGRESSIVISTS'
WHO BY PRECEPT AND EXAMPLE
ASSIST
THE INFAMOUS CAUSE
OF
EDUCATION WITHOUT RELIGION
AND WHO, BY PROMOTING THE IDEA, BORROWED FROM
FRENCH ATHEISM, OF DENYING TO THE
CHILDREN IN BOARD-SCHOOLS
AND ELSEWHERE,
THE KNOWLEDGE AND LOVE OF GOD,
AS THE TRUE FOUNDATION OF NOBLE LIVING,
ARE GUILTY
OF A WORSE CRIME THAN MURDER

INTRODUCTION

THE spirit, or soul, of a person is non-material, and so a factor 'beyond the range of ordinary knowledge'; which quotation comes from the definition of the word 'occult' as given in the Oxford Dictionary. Upon these grounds I feel justified in including this book by Marie Corelli in our Library; for it is the story of a young boy grappling with the problem of whether he has, or has not, a soul.

I must be frank. As was so often the case in this, then bestselling, author's day, the story, first published in 1896, positively drips with sentiment; but nevertheless it is well worth reading.

Lionel is the son of John Valliscourt Esq. of Valliscourt, the squire of a village in Somerset. He is typical of a great many Victorian fathers in that he is a grave man who considers it to be his natural right to dominate his household, and not even his beautiful wife dares to question his will. In that he was like my own father, who was always known in the household as 'the Master'; although, unlike Lionel's father who terrorised him, mine was very kind to me.

On the other hand, unlike most Victorian fathers, John Valliscourt was an atheist and his unbelief amounted to a fanatical hatred of all religions. No morning prayers for him, no church on Sundays; he would not even have a Bible in the house.

His one passion was the acquisition of knowledge, and Lionel, his only child, was the victim of it. Under a succession of tutors the poor boy swotted many hours every day. He was allowed no recreation, he was forbidden to go outside the grounds of the house, and mercilessly grilled every evening on his day's studies by his stern parent. Naturally, in learning, he became years beyond his age; but the price for it was poor health, a frail body and a joyless life.

He accepted both his lot and his father's atheism without complaint because he did not realise that either were unnatural. But one sunny day he did play truant. Scrambling through a hole in the garden hedge he crossed the fields to the village. Entering the churchyard he came upon the sexton, a Mr. Dale, digging a grave. With him was a lovely child – his little daughter Jessamine.

The sexton was a kindly, simple man and after the three of them had chatted for a while he asked the 'young gentleman' deferentially if he would like to go home with them for the evening meal. Lionel happily accepted and never in his life had he enjoyed anything so much as that high tea.

A few days later Jessamine crawls through the hedge bounding the Valliscourt garden to bring Lionel a bunch of wild flowers she has picked for him. Unknown to his father Lionel develops a clandestine friendship with the Dales. He falls in love with Jessamine and she with him. Love is the only word for it, although he is only eleven years old and she still a toddler; so it is the purest form of love.

I have always found the use of dialects or unusual pronunciation in books tiresome, and never use it in my own if it can possibly be avoided; but Marie Corelli's rendering of little Jessamine's prattle is superb. By it she portrays the personality of a little child with positively astounding clarity, and it is one of the principal joys of the book.

Naturally the Dales are regular church-goers and have an unshakable belief in the Christian faith. Little Jessamine is happy and fearless from her certainty that angels are always looking after her.

Lionel's association with the Dales leads to his beginning

to secretly question his father's atheism and the fanatical dogma that no one has a soul. Could it possibly be that he, Lionel, really has got a soul? He must find out – he must. Eventually he does.

Dennis Wheatley

CHAPTER 1

A HEAVY storm had raged all day on the north coast of Devon. Summer had worn the garb of winter in a freakish fit of mockery and masquerade; and even among the sheltered orchards of the deeply-embowered valley of Combmartin, many a tough and gnarled branch of many a sturdy apple-tree laden with reddening fruit, had been beaten to the ground by the fury of the blast and the sweeping gusts of rain. Only now, towards late afternoon, were the sullen skies beginning to clear. The sea still lashed the rocks with angry thuds of passion, but the strength of the wind was gradually sinking into a mere breeze, and a warm saffron light in the west showed where the sun, obscured for so many hours, was about to hide his glowing face altogether for the night behind the black vizor of our upward-moving earth. The hush of the gloaming began to permeate nature; flowers, draggled with rain, essayed to lift their delicate stems from the mould where they had been bowed prone and almost broken – and a little brown bird fluttering joyously out of a bush where it had taken shelter from the tempest, alighted on a window-sill of one of the nearest human habitations it could perceive, and there piped a gentle roundelay for the cheering and encouragement of those within before so much as preening a feather. The window was open, and in the room beyond it a small boy sat at a school-desk reading, and every now and then making pencil notes on a large folio sheet of paper beside him. He was intent upon his work – yet he turned quickly at the sound of the bird's song and listened, his deep thoughtful eyes darkening and softening with a liquid look as of unshed tears. It was only for a moment that he thus interrupted his studies – anon, he again bent over the book before him with an air of methodical patience and resignation strange to see in one so young. He might have been a bank clerk, or an experienced accountant in a London merchant's office, from his serious old-fashioned manner, instead of a child barely eleven years of age; indeed, as a matter of fact, there was an almost appalling expression of premature wisdom on his pale wistful features; – the 'thinking furrow' already marked his forehead – and what should still have been the babyish upper-curve of his sensitive little mouth, was almost, though not quite, obliterated by a severe line of constantly practised self-restraint. Stooping his fair curly head over the printed page more closely as the day darkened, he continued reading, pondering, and writing; and the bird, which had come to assure him as well as it could, that fine bright weather – such weather as boys love – might be expected tomorrow, seemed disappointed that its gay carol was not more appreciated. At any rate it ceased singing, and began to plume itself with fastidious grace and prettiness, peering round at the youthful student from time to time inquisitively, as much as to say – 'What wonder is this? The rain is over – the air is fresh – the flowers are fragrant – there is light in the sky – all the world of nature is glad, and rejoices – yet here is a living creature shut up with a book which surely God never had the making of ! – and his face is wan, and his eyes are sad, and he seems not to know the meaning of joy!'

The burning bars of saffron widened in the western heavens – shafts of turquoise-blue, pale rose, and chrysoprase flashed down towards the sea like reflections from the glory of some unbarred gate of Paradise – and the sun, flaming with August fires, suddenly burst forth in all his splendour. Full on Combmartin, with its grey old church, stone cottages, and thatched roofs overgrown with flowers, the cheerful radiance fell, bathing it from end to end in a shower of gold – the waves running into the quiet harbour caught the lustrous glamour and shone with deep translucent glitterings of amber melting into green – and through the shadows of the room where the solitary little student sat at work, a bright ray came dancing, and glistened on his bent head like the touch of some passing angel's benediction. Just then the door opened, and a young man entered, clad in white boating flannels.

'Still at it, Lionel!' he said kindly. 'Look here, drop it all for today! The storm is quite over; – come with me, and I'll take you for a pull on the water.'

Lionel looked up, half surprised, half afraid.

'Does *he* say I may go, Mr. Montrose?'

'I haven't asked him,' replied Montrose curtly, '*I* say you may – and not only that you may, but that you must! I'm your tutor – at least for the present – and you know you've got to obey me, or else ——!'

Here he squared himself, and made playfully threatening gestures after the most approved methods of boxing.

The boy smiled, and rose from his chair.

'I don't think I get on very fast,' he said apologetically, with a doubtful glance at the volume over which he had been poring – 'It's all my stupidity I suppose, but sometimes it seems a muddle to me, and more often still it seems useless. How, for instance, can I feel any real interest in the amount of the tithes that were paid to certain bishops in England in the year 1054? I don't care what was paid, and I'm sure I never shall care. It has nothing to do with the way people live nowadays, has it?'

'No – but it goes under the head of general information' – answered Montrose laughing – 'Anyhow, you can leave the tithes alone for the present – forget them – and forget all the bishops and kings too if you like! You look fagged out – what do you say to a first-class Devonshire tea at Miss Payne's?'

'Jolly!' and a flash of something like merriment lit up Lionel's small pale face – 'But we'll go on the water first, please! It will soon be sunset, and I love to watch a sunset from the sea.'

Montrose was silent. Standing at the open door he waited,

attentively observing meanwhile the quiet and precise movements of his young pupil, who was now busy putting away his books and writing materials. He did this with an almost painful care: wiping his pen, re-sharpening his pencil to be ready for use when he came back to work again, folding a scattered sheet or two of paper neatly, dusting the desk, setting up the volume concerning 'tithes' and what not, on a particular shelf, and looking about him in evident anxiety lest he should have forgotten some trifle. His tutor, though a man of neat taste and exemplary tidiness himself, would have preferred to see this mere child leaving everything in a disorderly heap, and rushing out into the fresh air with a wild whoop and bellow. But he gave his thoughts no speech, and studied the methodical goings to and fro of the patient little lad from under his half-drooped eyelids with an expression of mingled kindness and concern, till at last, the room being set in as prim an order as that of some fastidious old spinster, Lionel took down his red jersey-cap from its own particular peg in the wall, put it on, and smiled up confidingly at his stalwart companion.

'*Now*, Mr. Montrose!' he said.

Montrose started as from a reverie.

'Ah! That's it! Now's the word!'

Flinging on his own straw hat, and softly whistling a lively tune as he went, he led the way downstairs and out of the house, the little Lionel following in his footsteps closely and somewhat timidly. Their two figures could soon be discerned among the flowers and shrubs of the garden as they passed across it towards the carriage gate, which opened directly on to the high road – and a woman watching them from an upper window pushed her fair face through a tangle of fuchsias and called,

'Playing truant, Mr. Montrose? That's right! Always do what you're told not to do! Good-bye, Lylie!'

Lionel looked up and waved his cap.

'Good-bye, mother!'

The beautiful face framed in red fuchsia flowers softened at the sound of the child's clear voice – anon, it drew back into the shadow and disappeared.

The woods and hills around Combmartin were now all aglow with the warm luminance of the descending sun, and presently, out on the sea which was still rough, and sparkling with a million diamond-like points of spray, a small boat was seen, tossing lightly over the crested billows. William Montrose, B.A., 'oor Willie' as some of his affectionate Highland relatives called him, pulled at the oars with dash and spirit, and Lionel Valliscourt, only son and heir of John Valliscourt of Valliscourt in the county of Somerset, sat curled up, not in the stern, but almost at the end of the prow, his dreamy eyes watching with keen delight every wave that advanced to meet the little skiff and break against it in an opaline shower.

'I say, Mr. Montrose!' he shouted – 'This is glorious!'

'Aye, aye!' responded Montrose, B.A., with a deep breath and an extra pull – 'Life's a fine thing when you get it in big doses!'

Lionel did not hear this observation – he was absorbed in catching a string of seaweed, slimy and unprofitable to most people, but very beautiful in his eyes. There were hundreds of delicate little shells knitted into it, as fragile and fine as pearls, and every such tiny casket held a life as frail. Ample material for meditation was there in this tangle of mysterious organisms marvellously perfect, and while he minutely studied the dainty network of ocean's weaving, across the young boy's mind there flitted the dark shadow of the inscrutable and unseen. He asked within himself, just as the oldest and wisest scholars have asked to their dying day, the 'why' of things – the cause for the prolific creation of so many apparently unnecessary objects, such as a separate universe of shells for example – what was the ultimate intention of it all? He thought earnestly – and thinking, grew sorrowful, child though he was, with the hopeless sorrow of Ecclesiastes the Preacher and his incessant cry of '*Vanitas vanitatem!*' Meantime the heavens were ablaze with glory – the two rims of the friendly planets, earth and the sun, seemed to touch one another on the edge of the sea – then, the bright circle was covered by the dark and the soft haze of a purple twilight began to creep over the 'Hangman's Hills' as they are curiously styled – the Great and the Little Hangman. There is nothing about these grassy slopes at all suggestive of capital punishment, and they appear to have derived their names from a legend of the country which tells how a thief, running away with a stolen sheep tied across his back, was summarily and unexpectedly punished for his misdeed by the sheep itself, which struggled so violently, as to pull the cord that fastened it close round its captor's throat in a thoroughly 'hangman' like manner, thus killing him on the spot. The two promontories form a bold and pictures-que headland as seen from the sea, and Willie Montrose, resting for a moment on his oars, looked up at them admiringly, and almost with love in his eyes, just because they reminded him of a favourite little bit of coast scenery in his own more romantic and beautiful Scottish land. Then he brought his gaze down to the curled-up small figure of his pupil, who was still absorbed in the contemplation of his treasure-trove of seaweed and shells.

'What have you got there, Lionel?' he asked.

The boy turned round and faced him.

'Thousands of little people!' he answered, with a smile – 'All in pretty little houses of their own too – look!' and he held up his dripping trophy – 'It's quite a city, isn't it? – and I shouldn't wonder if the inhabitants thought almost as much of themselves as we do.' His eyes darkened, and the smile on his young face vanished. 'What do *you* think about it, Mr. Montrose? *I* don't see that we are a bit more valuable in the universe than these little shell-people.'

Montrose made no immediate reply. He pulled out a big silver watch and glanced at it.

'Tea-time!' he announced abruptly – 'Put the shell-people back in their own native element, my boy, and don't ask me any conundrums just now, please! Take an oar!'

With a flush of pleasure, Lionel obeyed – first dropping the seaweed carefully into a frothy billow that just then shouldered itself up caressingly against the boat, and watching it float away. Then he pulled at the oar manfully enough with his weak little arms – while Montrose, controlling his own strength that it might not overbalance that of the child, noted his exertions with a grave and somewhat pitying air. The tide was flowing in, and the boat went swiftly with it – the health-ful exercise sent colour into Lionel's pale cheeks and lustre into his deep-set eyes, so that when they finally ran their little craft ashore and sprang out of it, the boy looked as nature meant all boys to look, bright and happy-hearted, and the sad little furrow on his forehead, so indicative of painful thought and study, was scarcely perceptible. Glancing first up at the darkening skies, then at his own clothes sprinkled with salt spray, he laughed joyously as he said,

'I'm afraid we shall catch it when we get home, Mr. Mon-trose!'

'*I* shall – you won't;' returned Montrose imperturbably. 'But – as it's my last evening – it doesn't matter.'

All the mirth faded from Lionel's face, and he uttered a faint cry of wonder and distress.

'Your last evening? – oh no! – surely not! You don't – you can't mean it!' he faltered nervously.

Willie Montrose's honest blue eyes softened with a great tenderness and compassion.

'Come along, laddie, and have your tea!' he said kindly, his tongue lapsing somewhat into his own soft Highland accentua-tion; 'Come along and I'll tell you all about it. Life is like being out on the sea yonder – a body must take the rough with the smooth, and just make the best of it. One mustn't mind a few troubles now and then – and – and – partings and the like; you've often heard that the best of friends must part, haven't you? There now, don't look so downcast! – come along to Miss Payne's cottage, where we can get the best cream in all Devonshire, and we'll have a jolly spread and a talk out, shall we?'

But Lionel stood mute – the colour left his cheeks, and his little mouth once more became set and stern.

'I know!' he said at last, slowly, 'I know exactly what you have to tell me, Mr. Montrose! My father is sending you away. I am not surprised; oh no! I thought it would happen soon. You see you have been too kind – too easy with me – that's what it is. No – I'm not going to cry' – here he choked back a little rising sob bravely – 'you mustn't think that – I am glad you are going away for your own sake, but I'm sorry for myself – very sorry! I'm always feeling sorry for myself – isn't it cowardly? Marcus Aurelius says the worst form of cowardice is self-pity.'

'Oh, hang Marcus Aurelius!' burst out Montrose.

Lionel smiled – a dreary little cynical smile.

'Shall we go and have our tea?' he suggested quietly – 'I'm ready.'

And they walked slowly up from the shore together, – the young man with a light yet leisurely tread, the child with wearily dragging feet that seemed scarcely able to support his body. Painful thoughts and forebodings kept them silent, and they exchanged not a word, even when a sudden red and golden afterglow flashed across the sea as the very last salutation of the vanished sun – indeed they scarcely saw the fiery splendour that would, at a happier moment, have been a perfect feast of beauty to their eyes. Turning away from the principal street of the village they bent their steps towards a small thatched cottage, overgrown from porch to roof with climbing roses, fuchsias and jessamine, where an unobtrusive signboard might be just discerned framed in a wreath of brilliant nasturtiums, and bearing the following device

CLARINDA CLEVERLY PAYNE.

NEW LAID EGGS.   DEVONSHIRE CREAM.   JUNKETS.
TEAS PROVIDED.

Within this rustic habitation, tutor and pupil disappeared, and the pebbly shore of Combmartin was left in the possession of two ancient mariners, who, seated side by side on the overhanging wall, smoked their pipes together in solemn silence, and watched the gradual smoothing of the sea as it spread itself out in wider, longer, and more placid undulations, as though submissively preparing for the coming of its magnetic mistress, the moon.

CHAPTER 2

THAT same evening, John Valliscourt, Esquire of Valliscourt, sat late over his after-dinner wine, conversing with a languid, handsome-featured person known as Sir Charles Lascelles, Baronet. Sir Charles was a notable figure in 'swagger' society, and he had been acquainted with the Valliscourts for some time, in fact he was almost an 'old friend' of theirs, as social 'old friends' go, that phrase nowadays merely meaning about a year's mutual visiting, without any unpleasant strain on the feelings or the pockets of either party. Whenever the Valliscourts were in town for the season at their handsome residence in Grosvenor Place, Sir Charles was always 'dropping in', and dropping out again, a constant and welcome guest, a purveyor of fashionable scandals, and a thoroughly reliable informant concerning the ins and outs of the newest approaching divorce. But his appearance at Combmartin was quite unlooked-for, he having been supposed to have gone to his 'little place' (an estate of several thousand acres) in Inverness-shire. And it was concerning his present change of plan and humour that Mr. Valliscourt was just now rallying him in ponderously playful fashion.

'Ya-as!' drawled Sir Charles, in answer – 'I have doosid habits of caprice. Never know what I'm going to do from one day to another! Fact, I assure you! You see a chum of mine has got Watermouth Castle for a few weeks, and he asked me to join his house-party. That's how it is I happen to be here.'

Mrs. Valliscourt, who had left the dinner-table and was seated in a lounge chair near the open window, looked round and smiled. Her smile was a very beautiful one – her large flashing eyes and brilliantly white teeth gave it a sun-like dazzle that amazed and half bewitched any man who was not quite prepared to meet it.

'I suppose you are all very select at Watermouth,' – observed Mr. Valliscourt, cracking a walnut and beginning to peel the kernel with a deliberate, and fastidious nicety which showed off his long, white, well-kept fingers to admirable advantage – 'Nothing lower than a baronet, eh?'

And he laughed softly.

Sir Charles gave him a quick glance from under his lazily drooping eyelids that might have startled him had he perceived it. Malice, derision, and intense hatred were expressed in it, and for a second it illumined the face on which it gleamed with a wicked flash as of hell-fire. It vanished almost as quickly as it had shone, and a reply was given in such quiet, listless tones as betrayed nothing of the speaker's feelings.

'Well, I really don't know! There's a painter fellow staying with us – one of those humbugs called "rising artists," – gives himself doosid airs too. He's got a commission to do the castle. Of course he isn't thought much of – we keep him in his place as much as we can – still he's there, and he doesn't dine with the servants either. The rest are the usual lot – dowagers with marriageable but penniless daughters – two or three ugly "advanced" young women who have brought their bicycles and go tearing about the country all day and a few stupid old peers. It's rather slow. I was bored to exhaustion at the general tea-meeting this afternoon, so knowing you were here I thought I'd ride over and see you.'

'Delighted!' said Mr. Valliscourt, politely – 'But may I ask *how* you knew we were here?'

Sir Charles bit his lip to hide a little smile, as he answered lightly:

'Oh, everybody knows everything in these little out-of-the-way villages. Besides, when you take the only available large house in Combmartin you can't expect to hide your light under a bushel. It's really a charming old place too.'

'It's a barrack,' said Mrs. Valliscourt, speaking now for the first time, and looking straight at her husband as she did so, – 'It's excessively damp, and very badly furnished. Of course it could be made delightful if anybody were silly enough to spend a couple of thousand pounds upon it – but as it is, I cannot possibly imagine why John took such a horrid little hole for a summer holiday residence.'

'You know very well why I took it,' returned Mr. Valliscourt stiffly – 'It was not for my personal enjoyment, or for yours. I am old enough, I presume, to do without what certain foolish people call "a necessary change", and so are you for that matter. I was advised to give Lionel the benefit of sea-air – and as I was anxious to avoid the noise and racket of ordinary sea-side places, as well as the undesirable companionship of other people's children who might endeavour to associate with my son, I chose a house at Combmartin because I considered, and still consider, Combmartin perfectly suited for my purpose. Combmartin being off the line of railway and somewhat difficult of access, is completely retired and thoroughly unfashionable – and Lionel will be able to continue his holiday tasks under an efficient tutor without undue distraction or interruption.'

He said all this in a dry methodical way, cracking walnuts between whiles, with a curious air, as of coldly civil protest against the vulgarity of eating them.

Mrs. Valliscourt turned her head away, and looked out into the tangled garden, where the foliage, glistening with the day's long rain, sparkled in the silver gleam of the rising moon. Sir Charles Lascelles said nothing for a few moments – then he suddenly broke silence with a question. 'You are giving Montrose the sack aren't you?'

'I am dismissing Mr. Montrose – yes, certainly,' replied Valliscourt, his hard mouth compressing itself into harder lines – 'Mr. Montrose is too young for his place, and too self-opinionated. It is the fault of all Scotchmen to think too much of themselves. He is clever; I do not deny that; but he does not work Lionel sufficiently. He is fonder of athletics than classics. Now in my opinion, athletics are altogether overdone in England – and I do not want my son to grow up with all his brains in his muscles. His intellectual faculties must be developed –'

'At the expense of the physical?' interposed Sir Charles – 'Why not do both together?'

'That is my aim and intention,' – said Valliscourt somewhat pompously – 'but Mr. Montrose is not fitted either by education or temperament to carry out my scheme. In fact he has refused point-blank to go through the schedule of tuition I have formulated for the holiday tasks of my son, and has taken it upon himself to say to me – to *me*! – that Lionel is not capable of such a course of study, and that complete rest is what the boy requires. Of course this is an excuse to obtain a good time for himself in the way of boating and other out-of-door amusements. Moreover, I have discovered to my extreme concern, that Mr. Montrose has not yet thrown off the shackles of superstitious legend and observance, and that in spite of the advance of science, he is really not much better than a savage in his ideas of the universe. He actually believes in Mumbo-Jumbo – that is, God – still! – and also in the immortality of the soul!' Here Mr. Valliscourt laughed outright. 'Of course, if it were not so ridiculous, I should be angry – all the same, one cannot be too particular in the matter of a child's training and education, and I am considerably annoyed that I was not made aware of these barbarous predilections and prejudices of his before he took up a responsible position in my house.'

'Of course you would not have engaged him if you had known?' queried Sir Charles.

'Certainly not.' Here Mr. Valliscourt looked at his watch. 'Will you excuse me? It is nine o'clock, and I told Montrose to attend me at that hour in my study to receive the remaining portion of his salary. He leaves by the early coach tomorrow morning.'

Mrs. Valliscourt rose, and moved with an elegant languor towards the door.

'You had better come into the drawing-room, Sir Charles, and have a chat with *me*,' she said, favouring the baronet with one of her dazzling smiles as she glanced back at him over her shoulder – 'I suppose you are in no very special hurry to return to Watermouth?'

'No – not just immediately!' he replied with an answering smile, as he followed her out across the square oak-panelled hall and into the apartment she had named, which had the merit of being more comfortably furnished than any other part of the house, and moreover boasted four deep bay-windows, each one commanding different and equally beautiful views of the surrounding country. Mr. Valliscourt meantime went in an opposite direction, and entered a small parlour, formerly a storeroom, but now transformed into a kind of study, where he found William Montrose, B.A., awaiting him.

'Oor Willie' looked pale, and his lips were hard set. His employer nodded to him carelessly in passing, and then sitting down at his office-desk, unlocked a drawer, took from thence his cheque-book, and wrote out a sum that was more than 'oor Willie's' due. As he handed it over, the young man glanced at it, and coloured hotly.

'No thank you, Mr. Valliscourt,' – he said – 'The exact sum, please, and not a farthing over.'

'What!' exclaimed Valliscourt in a satirical tone – 'A Scotchman refuse an extra fee! Is this the age of miracles?'

Montrose grew paler, but kept himself quiet.

'Think what you like of Scotchmen, Mr. Valliscourt,' he returned, composedly – 'They can get on without your good opinion I daresay, and certainly they need none of my defending. I merely refuse to accept anything I have not honestly earned – there is no miracle in that, I fancy. It is not as if I took my dismissal badly – on the contrary, I should have dismissed myself if you had not forestalled me. I will have no share in child-murder.'

If a bomb had exploded in the little room, Mr. Valliscourt could not have looked more thoroughly astounded. He sprang from his chair and confronted the audacious speaker in such indignation as almost choked his utterance.

'Ch—ch—child-murder!' he spluttered, trembling all over in the excess of his sudden rage – 'D—d—did I hear you rightly, sir? Ch—child-murder!'

'I repeat it, Mr. Valliscourt!' – said Montrose, his blue eyes now flashing dangerously and his lips quivering – 'Child-murder! Take the phrase and think it over! You have only one child – a boy of a most lovable and intelligent disposition – quick-brained – too quick-brained by half! – and you are killing him with your hard and fast rules, and your pernicious "system" of intellectual training. You deprive him of such pastimes and exercises as are necessary to his health and growth – you surround him with petty tyrannies which make his young life a martyrdom – you give him no companions of his own age, and you are, as I say, murdering him – slowly perhaps, but none the less surely. Any physician with the merest superficial knowledge of his business, would tell you what I tell you – that is, any physician who preferred truth to fees.'

White with passion, Mr. Valliscourt snatched up the cheque he had just written and tore it into fragments – then opening another drawer in his desk, he took out a handful of notes and gold, and counting them rapidly, flung them upon the table.

'Hold your insolent tongue, sir!' he said in hoarse accents of ill-suppressed fury – 'There is your money – exact to a farthing; take it and go! And before you presume to apply for another situation as tutor to the son of a gentleman, you had better learn to know your place and put a check on your Scotch conceit and impertinence! Not another word! – go!'

With a sudden proud lifting of his head, Montrose eyed his late employer from heel to brow and from brow to heel again, in the disdainful 'measuring' manner known to fighting men – his eyes sparkled with anger – and his hands involuntarily clenched. Then all at once, evidently moved by some thought which restrained, if it did not entirely overcome his wrath, he swept up his wage lightly in one hand, turned and left the room without either a 'thank you' or 'good-evening'. When he had gone, John Valliscourt burst into an angry laugh.

'Insolent young cub!' he muttered – 'How such fellows get University honours and recommendations is more than I can imagine! Favouritism and jobbery I suppose – like everything else. An inefficient, boastful, lazy Scotchman if ever there were one! – and the worst companion in the world for Lionel. The boy has done nothing but idle away his time ever since he came. I'm very glad Professor Cadman-Gore is able to accept a few weeks of holiday tuition – he is expensive certainly – but he will remedy all the mischief Montrose has done, and get Lionel on; – he is a thoroughly reliable man, too, on the religious question.'

Soothed by the prospect of the coming of Professor Cadman-Gore, Mr. Valliscourt cooled down, and presently went to join his wife and Sir Charles Lascelles in the drawing-room. He found that apartment empty however, and on inquiry of one of the servants, learnt that Sir Charles had been gone some minutes, and that Mrs. Valliscourt was walking by herself in the garden. Mr. Valliscourt thereupon went to one of the deep bay-windows which stood open, and sniffed the scented summer air. The day's rain had certainly left the ground wet, and he was not fond of strolling about under damp trees. The moon was high, and very beautiful in her clear fullness, but Mr. Valliscourt did not admire moonlight effects – he thought all that kind of thing 'stagey'. The grave and devotional silence of the night hallowed the landscape – Mr. Valliscourt disliked silence, and he therefore coughed loudly and with much unpleasant throat-scraping, to disturb it. Throat-scraping gave just the necessary suggestion of prose to a picture which would otherwise have been purely romantic – a picture of shadowed woodland and hill and silver cloud and purple sky, in all of which beauteous presentments, mere humanity seemed blotted out and forgotten. Mr. Valliscourt coughed his ugly cough in order to get humanity into it – and as he finished the last little hawking note of irritating noise, he wondered where his wife was. The garden was a large and rambling one, and had been long and greatly neglected, though the owners of the place had shrewdly arranged with Mr. Valliscourt, when he had taken the house for three months, that he should pay a gardener weekly wages to attend to it. A decent but dull native of Combmartin had been elected to this post, and his exertions had certainly effected something in the way of clearing the paths and keeping them clean – but he was apparently incapable of dealing with the wild growth of sweet-briar, myrtle, fuchsia and bog oak that had sprung up everywhere in the erratic yet always artistic fashion of mother Nature, when she is left to design her own woodland ways – so that the entire pleasaunce was more a wilderness than anything else. Yet it had its attractions, or seemed to have, at least for Mrs. Valliscourt, for she passed nearly all her time in it. Now, however, owing to the long shadows, her husband could not perceive her anywhere, though presently as he stood at the window, he heard her voice carolling an absurd ditty, of which he caught a distinct fragment concerning

'Gay Bo-hem-i-*ah*!
We're not particular what we do
In gay Bo-hemi-i-*ah*" –

whereat, his face, cold and heavy-featured, as it was, grew downright ugly in its expression of malign contempt.

'She ought to have been a music-hall singer!' he said to himself with a kind of inward snarl – 'She has all the taste and talent required for it. And to think she is actually well-born and well educated! What an atrocious anomaly!'

He banged the window to violently, and went within. There was a smoking-room at the back of the house, and thither he retired with his cigar-case, and one of the dullest of all the various dull evening papers.

CHAPTER 3

EARLY the next morning between six and seven o'clock, little Lionel Valliscourt was up and dressed and sitting by his bedroom window, cap in hand, waiting eagerly for Montrose to appear. He was going to see his friendly tutor off by the coach, and the idea was not without a certain charm and excitement. It was a perfect day, bright with unclouded sunshine, and all the birds were singing ecstatically. The boy's sensitive soul was divided between sadness and pleasure – sadness at losing the companionship of the blithe, kindly, good-natured young fellow who alone, out of all his various teachers, had seemed to understand and sympathise with him – pleasure at the novelty of getting up 'on the sly' and slipping out and away without his father's knowledge, and seeing the coach, with its prancing four horses, its jolly driver, and its still jollier red-faced guard, all at a halt outside the funny old inn, called by various wags the 'Pack o' Cards' on account of its peculiar structure – and watching Mr. Montrose climb up thereon to the too-tootle-tooing of the horn, and then finally, beholding the whole glorious equipage dash away at break-neck speed to Barnstaple! This was something for a boy, as mere boy, to look forward to with a thrill of expectation; – but deep down in his heart of hearts he was thinking of another delight as well – a plan he had formed in secret, and of which he had not breathed a word, even to Willie Montrose. The scheme was a bold and dreadful one; and it was this – to run away for the day. He did not wish to shirk his studies – but he knew there were to be no lessons till his new tutor, Professor Cadman-Gore arrived, and Professor Cadman-Gore was not due till that evening at ten o'clock. The whole day therefore was before him – the long, beautiful, sunshiny day – and he, in his own mind, resolved that he would for once make the best of it. He had no wish to deceive his father – his desire for an 'escapade' arose out of an instinctive longing which he himself had not the skill to analyse – a longing not only for freedom, but for rest. Turning it over and over in his thoughts now, as he had turned it over and over all night, poor child, he could not see that there was any particular harm or mischief in his intention. Neither his father nor mother ever wanted him or sent for him except at luncheon, which was his dinner – all the rest of the time he was supposed to be with his tutor, always engaged in learning something useful. But now, it so happened that he was to be left for several hours without any tutor, and why should he not take the chance of liberty while it was offered him? He was still mentally debating this question, when Montrose entered softly, portmanteau in hand.

'Come along, laddie!' he said, with a kind smile – 'Step gently! Nobody's astir – and I'll aid and abet you in this morning's outing. We're going to breakfast together at Miss Payne's – the coach won't be here for a long time yet.'

Lionel gave a noiseless jump of delight on the floor, and then did as he was told, creeping after his tutor down the stairs like a velvet-footed kitten, and reddening with excess of timidity and pleasure when the big hall-door was opened cautiously and closed again with equal care behind them, and they stood together among the honey-suckle and wild-rose tangles of the sweetly-scented garden.

'Let me help you carry your portmanteau, Mr. Montrose' – he said sturdily – 'I'm sure I can!'

'I'm sure you can't!' returned Montrose, with a laugh, 'Leave it alone, my boy – it's too heavy for you. Here, you can carry my Homer instead!'

Lionel took the well-worn, leather-bound volume, and bore it along in both hands reverently as though it were a sacred relic.

'Where are you going, Mr. Montrose?' he asked presently – 'Have you got another boy like me to teach?'

'No – not yet. I wonder if I shall manage to find another boy like you, eh? Do you think I shall?'

Lionel considered seriously for a moment before replying.

'Well, I don't know,' he said at last – 'I suppose there must be some. You see when you're an only boy, you get different to other boys. You've got to try and be more clever, you know. If I had two or three brothers now, my father would want to make every one of them clever, and he wouldn't have to get it all out of me. That's how I look at it.'

'Oh, that's how you look at it,' echoed Montrose, studying with some compassion, the delicate little figure trotting at his side – 'You think your father wants to get the brain-produce of a whole family out of you? Well – I believe he does!'

'Of course he does!' averred Lionel, solemnly. 'And it is very natural if you think of it. If you've only got one boy, you expect a good deal from him!'

'Too much by half!' growled Montrose, *sotto voce* – then aloud he added – 'Well, laddie, you needn't fret yourself – you are learning quite fast enough, and you know a good deal more now than ever I did at your age. I was at school at Inverness when I was a little chap, and passed nearly all my time fighting – that's how I learned my lessons!'

He laughed – a joyous ringing laugh which was quite infectious, and Lionel laughed too. It seemed so droll for a boy to pass his time in fighting! – so very exceptional and extraordinary!

'Why, Mr. Montrose,' – he exclaimed – 'what did you fight so much for?'

'Oh, any excuse was good enough for me!' returned Montrose gleefully, 'If I thought a boy had too long a nose, I pulled it for him, and then we fought the question out together. They were just grand times! – grand!'

'I have never fought a boy,' – murmured Lionel regretfully, 'I never had any boy to fight with!'

Montrose looked down at him, and a sudden gravity clouded his previous mirth.

'Listen to me laddie,' he said earnestly – 'When you have a chance, ask your father to send you to school. You've a tongue in your head – ask him – say it's the thing you're longing for – beg for it as though it were your life. You're quite ready for it; you'll take a high place at once with what you know, and you'll be as happy as the day is long. You'll find plenty of boys to fight with – and to conquer! – fighting is the rule of this world, my boy, and to those who fight well, so is conquering. And it's a good thing to begin practising the business early – practice makes perfect. Tell your father – and tell this professor who is coming to take my place, that it is your own wish to go to a public school – Eton, Harrow, Winchester – any of them can turn out men.'

Lionel looked pained and puzzled.

'Yes – I will ask,' – he said – 'But I'm sure I shall be refused. Father will never hear of it. The boys in public schools all go to church on Sundays, don't they? Well, you know I should never be allowed to do *that*!'

Montrose made no reply, and they walked on in unbroken silence, till they reached the abode of Miss Clarinda Cleverly Payne, where on the threshold stood a bright-eyed, pleasant-faced, active personage in a lilac cotton gown and snow-white mob-cap of the fashion of half a century ago.

'Good-morning, sir! Nice morning! Good-morning, Master Lionel! Well now, toe be sure, I dew believe the eggs is just laid for you! I heerd the hens a-clucking the very minute you came in sight! Ah dearie me! If we all did our duty when it was expected of us, like my hens, the world would get on a deal better than it dew! Walk in, sir! – walk in, Master Lionel! – the table's spread and everything's ready; the window's open too, for there's a sight o' honeysuckle outside and it dew smell

32

sweet, I can assure you! Nothing like Devonshire honeysuckle except Devonshire cream! Ah, and you'll find plenty o' that for breakfast! And I'm sure this little gentlemen's sorry his kind master's going away, eh?'

'Yes, I am very sorry, ma'am,' said Lionel earnestly, taking off his little cap politely as he looked up at the worthy Clarinda's sunbrowned, honest countenance – 'But it isn't much use being sorry, is it? He must go, and I must stay – and if I were to fret for a whole year about it, it wouldn't make any difference would it?'

'No, that it wouldn't' – returned Miss Payne, staring hard into the pathetic young eyes that so wistfully regarded her – 'But you see some of us can't take things so sensibly as you do, my dear! – we're not all so clever!'

'Clever!' echoed Lionel, with an accent of such bitterness as might have befitted a cynic of many years' worldly experience – 'I'm not clever. I am only crammed.'

'Lord bless us!' exclaimed Clarinda, gazing helplessly about her – 'What does the child mean?'

'He means just what he says' – answered Montrose with a slight, rather sad smile – 'If you had to learn all the things Lionel is supposed to know —'

'Larn?' interrupted Miss Clarinda with a sharp sniff – 'Thank the Lord I ain't had no larnin'! I know how to do my work and live honestly without runnin' into debt – and that's enough for me. To see the young gels nowadays with their books an' their penny papers, all a-gabblin' of a parcel o' rubbish as doesn't consarn 'em – it dew drive me wild, I can tell you! My niece Susie got one o' them there cheap novels one day, and down she sat, a-readin' an' a-readin', an' she let the cream boil and spoilt it, an' later on in the day, she slipt and fell on the doorstep with a dozen new-laid eggs in her apron and broke eight o' them – then in a week or two she took to doin' her hair in all sorts o' queer towzley ways, and pinched her waist in, till she couldn't fancy her dinner and her nose got as red as a carrot. I said nothing – for the more you say to they young things the worse they get – but at last I got hold o' the book that had done the mischief and took to readin' it myself. Lor! – I laughed till I nearly split! – a parcel o' nonsense all about a fool of a country wench as couldn't do nothing but make butter, and yet she married a lord an' was took to Court with di'monds an' fal-lals! – such a muck o' lies was printed in that there book as was enough to bring the judgment of the Almighty on the jackass as wrote it! I went to my niece and I sez to her, sez I – "Susie my gel, you're a decent, strong, well-favoured sort o' lass, taken just as God made ye, and if you behave yourself, you may likely marry an honest farmer lad in time – but if ye get such notions o' lords and ladies as are in this silly lyin' book, an' go doin' o' your hair like crazy Jane, there's not a man in Combmartin as won't despise ye. An' ye'll go to the bad, my gel, as sure as a die!' She was a decent lass, Susie, an' she knew I meant well by her, so she just dropped the book down our old dry well in the back yard, seventy feet deep, and took to the cream again. She's married well now, and lives over at Woolacombe, very comfortably off. She's got a good husband, a poultry-farm and three babies, an' she's no time for novel-readin' now, thanks to the Lord!'

This narrative, delivered volubly with much oratorical gesture and scarcely any pauses, left Miss Clarinda well-nigh out of breath, and as she and her visitors were now in the one 'best parlour' of the cottage, she ceased talking, and bustled about to get them their breakfast. Montrose leaned out of the open lattice-window where the 'sight o' honeysuckle' hung in fragrant garlands, and inhaled the delicious perfume with a deep breath of delight.

'It's a bonnie place, this Devonshire' – he said, half to himself and half to Lionel – 'But it's not so bonnie as Scotland.'

Lionel had sat down in the window-nook with rather a weary air, the Homer volume still clasped in his hands.

'Are you going to Scotland soon?' he asked.

'Yes. I shall go straight home there for a few days and see my mother.' Here the young man turned and surveyed his small pupil with involuntary tenderness. 'I wish I could take you with me,' he added softly – 'My mother would love you, I know.'

Lionel was mute. He was thinking to himself how strange it would seem to be loved by Mr. Montrose's mother, as he was not loved by his own. At that moment, Clarinda Cleverly Payne brought in the breakfast in her usual smart, bustling way – excellent tea, new milk, eggs, honey, cream, jam, home-made bread, and scones smoking hot, were all set forth in tempting profusion and to crown the feast, an antique china basket filled with the rosiest apples and juiciest pears, was placed in the centre of the table. William Montrose, B.A., and his little friend sat down to their good cheer, each with very different feelings – 'oor Willie' with a hearty and appreciative appetite – the boy with only a faint sense of hunger, which was over-weighted by mental fatigue and consequent physical indifference. However he tried to eat well to please the kindly companion from whom he was so soon to be parted – and it was not till he had quite finished, that Montrose, pushing aside his cup and plate, addressed the following remarks to his late pupil:

'Look here, Lionel,' he said, 'I don't want you to forget me. If ever you should take it into your head to run away' – here a deep blush crimsoned Lionel's face, for was he not going to run away that very day? – 'or – or anything of that sort, just write and tell me all about it first. A letter will always find me at my mother's house, The Nest, Kilmun. I don't, of course, wish to persuade you to run away' – (he looked as if he did though!) 'because that would be a very desperate thing to do – still, if you feel you can't hold up under your lessons, or that Professor Cadman-Gore is too much for you, why, rather than break down altogether, you'd better show a clean pair of heels. I expect I'm giving you advice which a good many people would think very wrong on my part – all the same, boys *do* run away at times – it *has* been done!' Here his merry blue eyes twinkled. 'And if you have any more of that giddiness you complained of the other day – or if you go off in a dead faint as you did last week – you really mustn't conceal these sensations any longer – you must tell your father, and let him take you to see a doctor.'

Lionel listened with an air of rather wearied patience.

'What's the good of it?' he sighed – 'I'm not ill, you know. Besides I've had the doctor before, and he said there was nothing the matter with me. Doctors don't seem to be very clever – my mother was ill two years ago, and they couldn't cure her. When they gave her up and left her alone, she got well. Things always appear to go that way – the more you do, the worse you get.'

Montrose was quite accustomed to such a hopeless tone of reasoning from the boy – yet somehow, on this bright summer morning when he, in the full enjoyment of health and liberty, was going home to those who loved him, the absolute loneliness of this child's life and his pathetic resignation to it, smote him with a keener sense of pain than usual.

'And as for running away' – continued Lionel flushing as he spoke – 'I might do that perhaps for a few hours . . . but if I tried to run away for good and go for a sailor, which is what I should like, I should only be brought back – you know I should. And if I wrote to you about it, I should get you into dreadful trouble. You don't seem to think of all that, Mr. Montrose, but *I* think of it.'

'You think too much altogether,' – said Montrose, almost crossly – it vexed him to realise that this boy of barely eleven years was actually older and more reflective in mind than himself, a man of seven-and-twenty! – 'You are always thinking!'

'Yes' – agreed Lionel gravely, 'But then there's so much to think about in this world, isn't there!'

To this Montrose volunteered no answer. He sat, gazing at the dish of rosy apples in front of him with a brooding frown – and presently, Lionel laid one little cold trembling hand on his arm.

'But I shall never forget you – Willie!' he said, pausing before the name – 'You know you said I might call you Willie sometimes. You have been very good to me – you are the youngest tutor I have ever had – and the kindest – and though I can't keep all the lessons in my head, I can keep the kindness. I can indeed!'

He looked so small and fragile as he spoke, his sensitive little face a-quiver with emotion, and his soft eyes full of wistful affection and appeal, that Montrose was much inclined to give him a hearty kiss, just as he would have kissed a pretty baby. But he remembered in time all the dry morsels of so-called wisdom that had been packed into that little curly head – all the profound meditations of dead-and-gone philosophers that were stored in the recesses of that young mind – and he reflected, with an odd sense of humorous pity, that it would never do to kiss such a learned little man. So he gave him a couple of pleasant pats on the shoulder instead and answered – 'All right laddie! I know! Only just think now and again of what I've said to you, and when you're getting puzzled and dazed-like over your books, go into the fresh air and never mind the lessons – and if you get a thrashing for it, well – all I can say is, a thrashing is better than a sickness. Health's the grandest thing going – a far sight better than wealth.' At that moment the 'too-too-tootle' of the coach-horn came ringing towards them in a gay sonorous echo, and he started up. 'By Jove! I must be off! Miss Payne! Clarinda!'

'Now, if it isn't like your impudence, Mr. Montrose' – said Miss Payne, appearing at the doorway with her strong bare

37

arms dusty with the flour of the scones she had just been making, 'to be calling me Clarinda! Upon my word, I don't know what the gentlemen are coming to' – here she giggled and simpered in spite of her fifty-two years, as Montrose, nothing daunted, dropped more than the money due for the breakfast into her hand, and audaciously kissed her on the cheek – (he had no scruples about kissing *her*, oh no! not at all! – though he had about kissing Lionel) – 'Really they seem to be quite reckless nowadays – it was very different, I dew assure you, when I was a gel –'

'Oh no, it wasn't, Clarinda, I *dew* assure you!' laughed Montrose, with a playful mimicking of her voice and manner – 'It was just the same, and always will be the same to the crack of doom! Men will always be devils – and women – angels! Good-bye, Clarinda!'

'Good-bye, sir! A pleasant journey to you!' and Miss Payne bobbed up and down under her rose-covered porch, after precisely the same fashion in which the greatest ladies of the land make their 'dip' salutation to Royalty – 'Hope to see you here again some day, sir!'

'I hope so too!' he answered cheerily, waving one hand, while he grasped his portmanteau with the other, and walked with a swinging stride down the village street, followed by Lionel, to the 'Pack o' Cards' inn, where the coach had just arrived. It was a picturesque 'turn-out', with its four strong, sleek horses, its passengers, all rendered more or less bright-faced by the freshness of the morning air, its white-hatted coachman, and its jolly guard, who blew the horn more for the pleasure of blowing it than anything else – and Lionel surveyed it in a kind of sober rapture.

'You are glad to go, Mr. Montrose' – he said – 'You *must* be glad to go!'

'Yes, I am glad in one way' – replied Montrose, 'But I'm sorry in another. I'm sorry to leave you, laddie – I should like to be living here for awhile just to keep you out of harm's way.'

'Would you?' Lionel looked at him surprisedly. 'But I am never in the way of harm – nothing ever happens to me of any particular sort, you know. One day is just like another.'

'Well, good-bye!' and Montrose, having given over his portmanteau to the coach-guard, laid both his hands on the boy's fragile shoulders, 'When you get home, tell your father it was I who took you out with me this morning to see me off, and that if he wants to question me about it, he knows where a letter will find me. *I* take all the blame, remember! Good-bye, my dear wee laddie! – and – and – God bless you!'

Lionel's lips quivered, and the smile he managed to force was very suggestive of tears.

'Good-bye!' he said faintly.

'Too-too-too-tootle-too!' carolled the guard on his shining horn – and Montrose climbed nimbly up to his place on the top of the coach. The red-faced driver bent a severe eye on certain village children that were standing about, agape with admiration at himself and his equipage. 'Now then! Out of the way, youngsters!' There followed a general scrimmage, and the horses started. 'Too-too-tootle-too!' Up the village street they galloped merrily in the cheerful sunlight, their manes blown back by the dancing breeze.

"Good-bye! Good-bye!' shouted Montrose once more, waving his straw hat energetically to the solitary small figure left standing in the road.

But Lionel's voice could not now 'carry' far enough to echo the farewell, so he only lifted his little red cap once in response, the parting smile soon fading from his young face, and the worn pucker on his brow deepening in intensity. He stood motionless – watching till the last glimpse of the coach had vanished – then he started, as it were from a waking dream, and found that he still held the Homer volume – Montrose had forgotten it. Some of the village children were standing apart, staring at him, and he heard them saying something about the 'little gemmun livin' up at the big 'ouse.'

He looked at them in his turn; – there were two nice red-cheeked boys with red-cheeked apples in their hands – their faces were almost the counterpart of the apples in roundness and shininess. He would have liked to talk to them, but he felt instinctively that if he made any advances in this direction, they would probably be either timid or resentful – so he dismissed the idea from his mind, and went on his own solitary way. He was not going home – no – he was quite resolved to have a real holiday all to himself, before his new teacher arrived. And as he knew the ancient church of Combmartin was considered one of the chief objects of interest in the neighbourhood, and as, owing to his father's 'system' of education and ideas concerning religion or rather non-religion, he had been forbidden to visit it, he very naturally decided to go thither. And the tears he had resolutely kept back as long as Willie Montrose had been with him, now filled his eyes and dropped slowly, one by one, as he thought sorrowfully that now there would be no more pleasant tossings in an open boat on the sea – no more excursions into the woods for 'botany lessons' which had served as an excuse for many do-nothing but health-giving rambles, and the reading or reciting of stirring ballads such as 'The Battle of the Baltic', and 'Henry of Navarre', under the refreshing shade of the beautiful green trees – nothing of all this in future – nothing to look forward to but the dreaded society of Professor Cadman-Gore. Professor Cadman-Gore had a terrible reputation for learning – all the world was as one mighty jackass, viewed in the light of his prodigious and portentous intellect – and the young boy's heart ached under the oppression of his thoughts as he walked, with the lagging step and bent head of an old man, towards the wooden churchyard gate, lifted the latch softly, and went in, Homer in hand, to stroll about and meditate, Hamlet-wise, among the graves of the forgotten dead.

CHAPTER 4

Hushing his little footsteps instinctively as he went up the moss-grown path between the grassy graves that rose in suggestive hillocks on either side of him, he paused presently in front of an ancient tombstone standing aslant, on the top of which sat a robin redbreast contentedly twittering, and now and then called 'Sweet!' to its unseen mate. It was a fearless bird, and made no movement to fly away as Lionel approached. Just beneath its brown wings and scarlet bosom, the grey headstone had blossomed into green – tiny ferns and tufts of moss had managed to find roothold there, and spread themselves out in pretty sprays of delicate foliage over the worn and blackened epitaph below:

HEERE LYETH
YE EARTHLIE BODIE OF SIMON YEDDIE
Saddler in Combmartin
WHO DYED
FULLE OF JOYE AND HOPE TO SEE
HIS DEARE MASTER
CHRISTE
ON THE 17TH DAYE OF JUNE 1671
AGED 102.
'And He lodged in ye House of one Simon, a Tanner.'

With much difficulty Lionel made out this quaint inscription, standing, as he did, at some little distance off, in order not to frighten away the robin. He had to spell each word over carefully before he could understand it, and even when he had finally got it clear, it was still somewhat incomprehensible to his mind. And while he stood thinking about it, and wondering at the oddly chosen text which completed it, the robin redbreast suddenly flew away with an alarmed chirp, and a man's head, covered with a luxuriant crop of roughly curling white hair, rose, as it seemed, out of the very ground goblin-wise, and looked at him inquisitively. Startled, yet by no means afraid, Lionel stepped back a few paces.

'Hulloa!' said the head. 'Doan't be skeer'd, little zur! I be only a-diggin' fur Mother Twiley.'

The accent in which these words were spoken was extremely gentle, even musical, despite its provincial intonation – and Lionel's momentary misgiving was instantly dispelled. Full of curiosity, he advanced and discovered the speaker to be a big, broad-shouldered, and exceedingly handsome man, the bulk of whose figure was partially hidden in a dark, squarely-cut pit of earth, which the boy's instinct told him was a grave.

'I'm not scared at all, thank you' – he said, lifting his little red cap with the politeness which was habitual to him – 'It was only because your head came up so suddenly that I started; I did not know anybody was here at all except the robin that flew away just now. What a big hole you are making!'

'Aye!' And the man smiled, his clear blue eyes sparkling with a cheery light as he turned over and broke a black clod of earth with his spade – 'Mother Twiley allus liked plenty o' room! Lor' bless 'er! When she was at her best, she 'minded me of a haystack – a comfortable, soft sort o' haystack for the chillern to play an' jump about on – an' there was allus chillern round her for the matter o' that. Well! Now she's gone, there's not a body as has got a word agin her, an' that's more than can be said for either kings or queens.'

'Is she dead?' asked Lionel softly.

'Why, yes, s'fur as this world's consarned, she's dead,' was the reply – 'But, Lord! what's this world! Nuthin'! Just a breath, an' we're done wi't. It's the next world we've got to look to, little zur – the next world is what we should all be a-workin' fur day an' night.

42

> ' "There's a glory o' the moon
> An' a glory o' the stars
> But the glory o' the angels shines
> Beyond our prison bars!" '

He sang this verse melodiously in a rich sweet baritone,
digging the while and patting the sides of the grave smooth
as he worked.

Lionel sat down on one of the grassy mounds and stared
at him thoughtfully.

'How can you believe all that nonsense?' he asked, with
reproachful solemnity – 'Such a big man as you are too!'

The grave-digger stopped abruptly in his toil, and turning
round, surveyed the little lad with undisguised astonishment.

'How can I believe all that nonsense!' he repeated at last
slowly – 'Nonsense! Is a wee mousie like you a-talkin' o' the
blessed sure an' certain hope o' heaven as *nonsense*? God ha'
mercy on ye, ye poor little thing! Who has had the bringin'
of ye up, anyway?'

Lionel flushed deeply and his eyes smarted with repressed
tears. He was very lonely; and he wanted to talk to this
cheery-looking man who had such a soft musical voice and
such a kindly smile, but now he feared he had offended him.

'My name is Lionel – Lionel Valliscourt,' he said in low,
rather tremulous tones – 'I am the only son of Mr. Valliscourt
who has taken the big house over there for the summer – that
one – you can just see the chimneys through the trees' –
and he indicated the direction by a little wave of his hand –
'And I have always had very clever men for tutors ever since
I was six years old – I shall be eleven next birthday – and they
have taught me lots of things. And why I said the next world
was nonsense was because I have always been told so. One
would be very glad, of course, if it were true, but then, it
isn't true. It is only an idea – a sort of legend. My fathers says
nobody with any sense nowadays believes it. Scientific books

prove to you, you know, that when you go into a grave like that,' and he pointed to the hole in which the white-haired sexton stood, listening and inwardly marvelling – 'you are quite dead for ever – you never see the sun any more, or hear the birds sing, and you never find out why you were made at all, which I think is very curious, and very cruel; and you are eaten up by the worms. Now it surely *is* nonsense, isn't it, to think you can come to life again after you are eaten by the worms? – and that is what I meant, when I asked how you could believe such a thing. I hope you will excuse me – I didn't wish to offend you.'

The grave-digger still stood silent. His fine resolute features expressed various emotions – wonder, pain, pity, and something of indignation – then, all at once these flitting shadows of thought melted into a sunny smile of tenderness.

'Offend me? No indeed! – ye couldn't do that, my little zur, if ye tried – ye're too much of a babby. An' so ye're Mr. Valliscourt's son, eh? – well, I'm Reuben Dale, the verger o' th' church here, an' sexton, an' road-mender, an' carpenter, an' anything else wotsoever my hand finds to do, I does it with my might, purvided it harrums nobody an' gits me a livin'. Now ye see these arms o' mine' – and he raised one of the brown muscular limbs alluded to – 'They ha' served me well – they ha' earned bread an' clothing, an' kep' wife an' child, an' please God they'll serve me yet many a long day, an' I'm grateful to have 'em for use an' hard labour – but I know the time'll come when they'll be laid down in a grave like this 'ere, stark an' stiff an' decayin' away to the bone, a-makin' soil fur vi'lets an' daisies to grow over me. But what o' that? I'll not be a'wantin' of 'em then – no more than I'm a-wantin' now the long clothes I wore when our passon baptised me at t' old font yonder. I, who am, at present, owner o' these arms, will be zumwheres else – livin' and thinkin', an' please the Lord, workin' too, for work's divine an' wholesome – I'll 'ave better limbs mebbe, an' stronger – but whatsever body

44

I get into, ye may depend on't, little zur, it'll be as right an' fittin' for the ways o' the next world, as the body I've got now is right an' fittin' fur this one. An' my soul will be the same as keeps me up at this moment, bad or good – onny I pray it may get a bit wiser an' better, an' not go down like.' He raised his clear blue eyes to the bright expanse above him, and murmured half inaudibly – '*Let him that thinketh he standeth, take heed lest he fall*' – and seemed for a moment lost in meditation.

'Please, Mr. – Mr. Dale, what do you mean by your soul?' asked Lionel gravely.

Reuben Dale brought his rapt gaze down from the shining sky to the quaint and solemn little figure before him.

'What do I mean, my dear?' he echoed, with a note of compassion vibrating in his rich voice – 'I mean the onny livin' part o' me – the "vital spark o' heavenly flame" in all of us, that our dear Lord died to save. That's what I mean – an' that's what you'll mean too, ye poor pale little chap, when ye'se growed up and begins to understand all the marvels o' God's goodness to us ungrateful sinners. Onny to think o' the blessed sunshine should be enough fur the givin' o' thanks – but Lord pity us! – we're sore forgetful of our daily mercies!'

'And – your friend – Mother Twiley,' – hinted Lionel, almost deferentially – 'Had she what you call a soul?'

'Aye, that she had! – an' a great one, an' a true one, an' an angel one – fur all that she wor old, an' not so well-looking in her body as she must ha' been in her mind' – replied the sexton, 'But ye may be sure God found her right beautiful in His sight when He tuk her to Himself t'other evening just as the stars were risin'.'

'But how do you know,' – persisted Lionel, who was getting deeply, almost painfully interested in the conversation – 'Do tell me please! – how do you *know* she had a soul?'

'My dear, when you see a very poor old woman, with

nothing of world's comfort or world's goods about her, bearing a humble an' hard lot in peace an' contentment, wi' a cheerful face an' bright eye, a smile fur every one, a heart fur the childer, forgiveness fur the wrongdoers, an' charity fur all, who can look back on eighty years o' life with a "Praise God" for every breath of it, you may be sure that somethin' better an' higher than the mere poor, worn, tired body o' her, keeps 'er firm to 'er work an' true to her friends – an' so 'twos with Mother Twiley. So fur as her body went, 'twos just a trouble to her – twitched wi' rheumatiz, an' difficult to manage in the matter o' mere breathing – but her soul was straight enough, an' strong enough. Lord! – 'ere in Combmartin we knew her soul so well that we forgot all about the poor old case it lived in – I hardly think we saw it! Our bodies are weak bothersome things, my dear – an' without a soul to help 'em along we should never keep 'em going.'

'I believe that,' – said Lionel, heaving a little sigh – 'I can't help believing it, though it's not what I've been taught. My body is weak; it aches all over often. Still, I think, Mr. Dale, that souls, such as you talk about, must be exceptions, you know. Like blue eyes, for instance – everybody hasn't got blue eyes; well, perhaps everybody hasn't got a soul. You see that might be how it is. My father would be very angry if you told him he had a soul. And I know he will never let *me* have one, not even if I could grow it some how.'

Reuben Dale was speechless. He gazed at the boy's small sad face in wonder too great for words. Himself a simple-hearted God-fearing man, who had lived all his life at Combmartin, working hard for his daily bread, and entirely contented with his humble lot, he had never heard of the feverish and foolish discussions held in over-populated cities, where deluded men and women shut out God from their consciences as they shut out the blue sky by the toppling height and close crowding together of their hideous houses – where the very press teaches blasphemy and atheism, and permits

46

to pass into the hands of the public, with praise and recommendation, such lewd books as might move even a Rabelais to sick abhorrence. And he certainly had never deemed it possible that any form of government could exist in the world which favoured the bringing-up and education of children without religion. He had heard of France – but he was not aware that it had eschewed religion from its public schools, and was rapidly becoming a mere forcing-bed for the production of child-thieves, child-murderers, and child-parricides. He believed in England as he believed in God, with that complete and glorious faith in mother-country which makes the nation great – and it would have been a shock to his steadfast, deeply religious nature, had he been told that even this beloved England of ours, misled by those who should have been her best guardians, was accepting lessons from France in open atheism, 'Simianism', and general 'free' morality. Thus, the child that sat before him was a kind of unnatural prodigy to his sight – the little pale face, framed in an aureole of fair curling hair, might have aptly fitted an angel – but the elderly manner, the methodical, precise fashion in which this young thing spoke, seemed to honest Reuben 'uncanny', and he ruffled his beard with one hand in dire perplexity, quite taken aback, and at a loss how to continue the conversation. For how could he give any instruction in the art of 'growing' a soul? Happily however, a diversion here occurred in the sudden, almost noiseless approach of a tiny girl, with the prettiest little face imaginable, that peered out like a pink rose from under a white 'poke' sun-bonnet and a tangle of nut-brown curls – a little girl who appeared to Lionel's eyes like a vision of Helen of Troy in miniature, so lovely and dainty was her aspect. He had never been allowed to read any fairy-tales, so he could not liken her to a fairy, which would have been more natural – but he had done a lot of heavy translation work in Homer, and he knew that all the heroes in the 'Iliad' quarrelled about this Helen, and that she was very beautiful. Therefore he immediately decided that Helen of Troy when she was a little girl (she must have been a little girl once!) was exactly like the charming small person who now came towards him, carrying a wicker basket on her arm, and tripping across graves as delicately as though she were nothing but a blossom blow over them by the summer breeze.

'Halloa!' exclaimed Reuben Dale, throwing down his spade, 'Here's my little 'un! Well, my Jas'min flower! Bringin' a snack for th' old feyther?'

At this query the little girl smiled, creating a luminous effect beneath her poke-bonnet as though a sunbeam were caught within it – then she made a small round O of her tiny red mouth, with the evident intention to thereby convey a hint of something delicious. And finally she opened her basket, and took out a brown jug, full of hot fragrant coffee, lavishly frothed at the top with cream, and two big slices of home-made bread and butter.

'Is that right, feyther?' she inquired, as she carefully set these delicacies on the edge of the grave within her father's reach.

'That's right, my bird!' responded Reuben, lifting her in his arms high above his head, and giving her a sounding kiss on both her rosy cheeks as he put her down again – 'An' look 'ere, Jessamine, there's a little gemmun for ye to talk to. Go an' say how-d'y-do to 'im.'

Thus commanded, Jessamine obeyed, strictly to the letter. She went to where Lionel sat admiringly watching her, and put out her dumpy mite of a hand.

'How-d'y-do!' said she. And before Lionel could utter a word in reply she had shaken her curls defiantly, and run away! The boy sprang up, pained and perplexed; Reuben Dale laughed.

'After her, my lad! Run! – the run'll do ye good! She's just like that at first – fur all the world like a kitten, fond o' fun! Ye'll find 'er a-hidin' round the corner!'

Thus encouraged, Lionel ran – actually ran – a thing he very seldom did. He became almost a hero, like the big men of the 'Iliad'! *His* 'Helen' was 'a-hidin' round the corner' – he was valiantly determined to find her – and after dodging the little white sun-bonnet round trees and over tombs till he was well-nigh breathless, she, like all feminine things condescended to be caught at last, and to look shyly in the face of her youthful captor.

'What boy be you?' she asked, biting the string of her sun-bonnet with an air of demure coquetry – 'You be prutty – all th' boys roond 'ere be oogly!'

Oh, what an accent for a baby 'Helen of Troy'! – and yet how charming it was to hear her say 'oogly', because she made another of those little round O's of her mouth that suggested deliciousness; – even the deliciousness of kissing. Lionel thought he would like to kiss her, and coloured hotly at the very idea. Meanwhile his 'Helen of Troy' continued her observation of him.

'Would 'ee like an apple?' she demanded, producing a small, very rosy one from the depths of a miniature pocket – 'I'll gi' ye this, if s'be ye'se let me bite th' red bit oot.'

If ever a young lady looked 'fetching' as the slang phrase expresses it, Miss Jessamine Dale did so at that moment. What with the mischievous light in her dark blue eyes, and the smile on her little mouth as she suggested that she should 'bite the red bit', and the altogether winsome, provocative, innocent allurement of her manner, Lionel quite lost his head for the moment, and forgot everything but the natural facts that he was a little boy, and she was a little girl. He laughed merrily – such a laugh as he had not enjoyed for many a weary day – and taking the apple from her hand, held it to her lips while she carefully closed her tiny teeth on the 'red bit' and secured it, the juice dropping all over her dimpled chin.

'I'm to have the rest, am I?' said Lionel, then, venturing

to hold her by the arm and assist her over a very large and very ancient grave, wherein reposed, as the half-broken tombstone said, 'Ye Bodie of Martha Dumphy, Aged Ninety-seven Yeeres.' Long, long ago lived Martha Dumphy – long, long ago she died – but could anything of her have still been conscious, she would have felt no offence or sacrilege in the tread of those innocent young feet that sprang so lightly over her last resting-place.

'Yes, you're to 'ave the rest' – replied Jessamine benevolently – then with an infinite slyness and humour she added – 'I've got 'nuther i' my poacket!'

How they laughed, to be sure! Forgetful of 'Ye Bodie of Martha Dumphy' they sat down on the grass that covered her old bones, and enjoyed their applies to the full, Miss Jessamine generously bestowing the 'red bit' of the second apple on Lionel, who, though he was not really hungry, found something curiously appetising in these stray morsels of juicy fruit lately plucked from the tree.

'Coom into th' church' – then said Jessamine, 'Feyther's left the door open. Coom an' see th' big lilies on th' Lord's table.'

Lionel looked into her lovely little face, feeling singularly embarrassed by this invitation. He knew what she meant of course – he had been duly instructed in the form of the Christian 'myth', as a myth only, in company with all the other creeds known to history. They had been bracketed together for his study and consideration in a group of twelve, thus:

1. Of Phta, and the Egyptian mythology.
2. Of Brahma, Vishnu and the Hindoo cults.
3. Of the Chaldean and Phoenician creeds.
4. Of the Greek and Roman gods.
5. Of Buddha and Buddhism.
6. Of Confucius and the Chinese sects.
7. Of the Mexican mythology.
8. Of Odin and the Norse beliefs.

9. Of Mohammedanism and the Koran.

10. Of the Talmud, and Jewish tradition.

11. Of Christ, and the gradual founding of the Christian myth on the relics of Greek and Roman Paganism.

12. Of the Advance of Positivism and Pure Reason, in which all these creeds are proved to be without foundation, and merely serving as obstacles to the Intellectual Progress of Man.

The above 'schedule' had formed a very special and particular part of Lionel's education, and he had been carefully taught that only semi-barbarians believed nowadays in anything divine or supernatural. The intellectual classes fully understood, so he was told, that there was no God, and that the First Cause of the universe was merely an Atom, productive of other atoms which moved in circles of fortuitous regularity, shaping worlds indifferently, and without any Mind-force whatever behind the visible matter. Thus had the intellectual classes fathomed the Eternal, entirely to their own satisfaction – and of course, he poor little Lionel, was being brought up to take his place among the intellectual classes, where his father was already a shining light of dogmatic pedantry. He was assured that only the poor, the ignorant, and the feeble-minded still appealed to God as 'Our Father', and believed in the socialist workman, Jesus of Nazareth, as a Divine Personage whose way of life and death had shown all men the road to Heaven. One of the chief faults found with Willie Montrose as a tutor, had been his implicit faith in these supernatural things, and his point-blank refusal to teach his young pupil otherwise. Hence the subject, Religion, had been removed altogether from Lionel's 'course of study,' and the unswerving firmness Montrose had shown on the matter had led, among other more trifling drawbacks, to his dismissal. All this was fresh in the boy's mind – and now Jessamine said 'Coom an' see th' big lilies on th' Lord's table!' She, then, was one of the 'semi-barbarians', this pretty little girl – and yet how happy she seemed! – what an innocent, dove-like expression of tenderness and trust shone in her eyes as she spoke! How very young she was! – and alas, how very old he felt as he looked at her! She knew so little – he had learned so much, and though he was but four years her senior, he seemed in his own pained consciousness to be an elderly man studying the merry pranks of a child.

'Coom!' repeated Jessamine – her 'coom' sounding very like the soft note of a ring-dove, as she got up from the grassy bed of 'Martha Dumphy's' everlasting sleep – 'It be cool i' th' church – we'll sit i' th' poopit an' y' shall tell me a story 'bout Heaven. Y' know all 'bout angels, don't 'ee? How they cooms down all in white an' kisses us when we'se in bed asleep? Did ever any of 'em kiss 'ee?'

Lionel's lonely little heart beat strangely. An angel kiss him! – what a sweet fancy – but how foolish! Yet with Jessamine's face so near his own he could not tell her that he did not believe in angels, she looked so like a little one herself. So he answered her quaint question with a simple 'No!'

'I would ha' thowt they did,' – continued Jessamine, encouragingly – 'Ye bain't a bad boy, be ye?'

Lionel smiled rather plantively.

'Perhaps I am' – he said – 'and perhaps that's why the angels don't come.'

'My mother's an angel,' went on Jessamine. 'She couldn't abear bein' away from God no longer, an' so she flew to Heaven one night quite suddint, with big white wings an' a star on her head. Feyther says she often flies doon jes' for a minute like, an' kisses 'im, an' me too, when we'se asleep. Auntie Kate takes care of us since she went.'

'Then she is dead?' queried Lionel.

'Nowt o' that' – replied Jessamine, peacefully. 'Hasn't I told 'ee she's an angel?'

'But have you ever seen her since she went away?' persisted the boy.

'No. I bain't good enough' – and a small sigh of pathetic self-reproach heaved the baby breast – 'I'se very little yet, an' bad offen. But I'll see her some day for sure.'

Lionel could find nothing to say to this, and in another minute they had entered the church together. The subtle sweet fragrance of the 'big lilies on th' Lord's table' came floating towards them on a cool breath of air as the heavy old oaken door swung open and closed again, and they paused in the aisle, hand in hand, looking gravely up and down – first at the tall white flowers that filled the gilt vases on either side of the altar, mystically suggesting in their snowy stateliness, the words 'Blessed are the pure in heart, for they shall see God'; – then, at the patterns of blue, red and amber cast on the stone pavement by the reflections of the sun through the stained-glass windows. The ancient roof, with its crookedly planned oak mouldings of the very earliest English style of architecture, had a grave and darkening effect on the sunshine, and the solemn hush of the place, expressive of past prayer, impressed Lionel with a sweet, yet unfamiliar sense of rest. Jessamine grasped his hand closer.

'Coom into th' poopit' – she whispered – 'There be soft cushions there an' a big big Bible – I'll show 'ee a pictur' – here she opened her eyes very wide – '*my* pictur! – my own very best pictur!'

Somewhat curious to see this treasure, Lionel climbed with her up the pulpit-stairs, feeling that he was really having what might be called an adventure on this his stolen holiday. Jessamine was evidently quite familiar with the pulpit as a coign of vantage, for she hauled the big Bible she had spoken of out of its recess with much care and much breathless labour, and placed it on a velvet cushion on the floor. Then she curled herself down beside it and, turning over a few pages, beckoned Lionel to kneel and look also.

'Here 'tis!' she said with a soft chuckle of rapture – 'See! See this prutty boy ! – you's somethin' a bit like, aint'y ?

An' see all these oogly ole men! They'se wise people, so they thinks. An' th' prutty boy's tellin' 'em how silly they be, an' aw' in a muddle wi' their books an' larnin' – an' how good God is, an' all 'bout Heaven – see! An' they'se very angry wi'm an' 'stonished, 'cos He's onny a boy, an' they'se all ole men as cross as sticks. An' there He is y'see, an' He knows all about what they oogly men doan't know, 'cos He's the little Jesus.'

The subject of the picture was Christ expounding the law to the doctors of the Temple, and Lionel studied it with an almost passionate interest. Only a boy! – and yet in His boyhood He was able to teach the would-be wise men of His day! 'Though,' thought Lionel, with his usual melancholy cynicism, 'perhaps they were not really wise, and that is why He found it easy.'

Meanwhile Jessamine having gloated over her 'own best pictur' sufficiently, shut the book, put it religiously back in its place, and sat herself down beside her companion on the top step of the pulpit-stair.

'Wot's y' name?' she demanded.

'Lionel,' he answered.

'Li'nel? How funny! Wot's Li'nel? 'Tain't a flower?'

'No. *Your* name is a flower.'

' 'Iss! Our jess'mine tree was all over bloom the mornin' I was born, an' that's why I'm called Jessamine. I likes my name better'n your'n.'

'So do I,' said Lionel smiling – 'Mine is not nearly such a pretty name. My mother calls me Lylie.'

'I likes that – that's prutty – I'se call'y Lylie, too,' declared Miss Jessamine promptly, and as she spoke she slipped an arm confidingly round his neck – 'You be a nice boy, Lylie! Now tell me a story!'

CHAPTER 5

LIONEL gazed at her in deeper perplexity than ever. What story could he tell her? He knew none that was likely to charm or interest a creature so extremely young. It was very delightful to feel her warm chubby arm round his neck, and to see her dear little face so close to his own, and he thought, as he looked, that he had never seen such beautiful blue eyes before, not even his mother's, which he had, till now, considered beautiful enough. But Jessamine's eyes had such heavenly sweetness in their liquid depths, and something moreover beyond mere sweetness – the untroubled light of a spotless innocence such as sometimes makes the softly-tinted cup of a woodland flower remind one involuntarily of a child's eyes. Only a very few flowers convey this impression – the delicate azure circle of the hepatica – the dark purple centre of the pansy – the pensive blue of the harebell – the frank smiling tint of the forget-me-not, or the iris-veined heart of the Egyptian lotus. But the child-look is in such blossoms, and we often recognise it when we come suddenly upon them peering heavenwards out of the green tangles of grass and fern. Jessamine's eyes were a mixture of grave pansy-hues and laughing forget-me-nots, and when she smiled both these flowers appeared to meet with a pretty rivalry in her shining glances. And once again Lionel thought of Helen of Troy.

'Ain't 'ee got no story?' quoth she presently, after waiting a patient two minutes – 'What book be that there?'

And she put a dumpy little red finger on the copy of Homer left behind by Willie Montrose and still carried under Lionel's arm.

'It's Homer,' replied the boy promptly – 'My tutor went away by the first coach this morning and he forgot to take it

with him. It's his book, and a favourite copy – I must send it
to him by post.'

' 'Iss – 'ee must send it to him,' echoed Jessamine approv-
ingly – 'What be 'Omer?'

'He was a great poet – the first great poet that ever lived,
so far as history knows, and he was an ancient Greek' –
explained Lionel – 'He lived – oh, ages ago. He tells all
about the Trojan wars in this book; it's an epic.'

'What's epik?' inquired Jessamine – 'An' what's Drojunwors?'

Lionel laughed softly. The gravity of the old church roof
hung over him, otherwise his laughter would have been less
restrained.

'You wouldn't understand it, if I told you, dear,' he said,
becoming suddenly protective and manful as he realised her
delightful ignorance and weakness – 'Homer was a poet –
do you know what poetry is?'

' 'Iss – 'deed I do!' declared Jessamine, allowing her head
to droop caressingly on his shoulder, 'I've 'eerd a lot o't.
I'll tell you some – it be like this:

> ' "Gentle Jesus meek an' mild,
>   Look upon a little child,
>   Pity my simplicitie
>   An' suffer me to come to Thee!" '

She looked up as she finished the familiar stanza with one
of her radiant baby smiles.

'Didn't I say that nice?' she demanded.

'Very nice!' murmured Lionel, while thoughts were flying
round and round in his brain concerning the 'semi-barbarians
who still believed in the Christian myth,' which was one of
his father's constantly repeated and favourite phrases.

'Now tell me some more 'Omer an' Drojunwors,' she said,
nestling against him like a soft kitten – 'Is it 'bout angels?'

'No,' replied Lionel – 'It is all about great big men – *very* big men — '

'Too big to get into this church?' queried Jessamine in awe-struck tones.

'Yes – I believe they would have been too big to get into this church' – said Lionel, smiling involuntarily – 'And they all fought about a lady called Helen, who was the most beautiful woman in the world.'

'Why did she let 'em fight?' asked Jessamine gravely – 'She was not a good lady to let the poor big men fight an' 'urt theirselves for 'er. She should 'ave made 'em all friends.'

'She couldn't' – said Lionel – 'You see they *wouldn't* be friends.'

'They must ha' been funny big men!' murmured Jessamine – 'Where be they all now?'

'Oh, dead ever so long ago!' laughed the boy – 'Some people say they never lived at all!'

'Oh, then it's all fairy-tale like Puss-in-Boots,' said Jessamine – 'Your Drojunwors is a fairy-book like mine. Only I like Puss-in-Boots better. Do'ee know *my* fairy-book?'

Lionel had never had what is called a 'fairy-book' in his life, fairy-books having been considered by his father in the same light as that with which Mr. H. Holman, one of Her Majesty's Inspectors of Schools recently regarded them, publicly denouncing them as 'dangerous to morality and mischievous as to knowledge, contradicting the most obvious and elementary facts of experience.' (Alas, good Dry-as-Dust Holman! How much thou art to be pitied for never having been in the least young! And dost thou not realise that Religion itself in all its forms of creed, 'contradicts the most obvious and elementary facts of experience'?) The little Lionel was unacquainted with Mr. Holman, but he knew his own fathers' stern contempt for fairy-tales, even for those which have, in many cases, strangely foretold some of the most brilliant recent discoveries in science, so he replied to Jessamine's question by a negative shake of his head, the while he gazed admiringly at the nut-brown curls that rippled in charming disarray on his shoulder.

'I'll tell 'ee somethin' in it,' – she continued, with the thinking dreamy air of a child-angel rapt in some sublime reverie – 'There wos once a little girl an' little boy – 'bout 's big as we be – they wos good an' prutty, an' they'd got a bad, bad ole uncle. He couldn't abide 'em 'cos they wos s' good an' 'e wos s' bad; so one day 'e took 'em out in a great big dark wood where no sun couldn't shine, an' there 'e lost 'em both. An' when they wos lost, they walked 'bout, up an' down, an' couldn't get out nohow, an' they got tired an' 'ungry, an' so they laid down an' said their prayers, an' put their arms round each other's necks – so – ' and here Jessamine cuddled closer – 'an' died jest right off, an' God took 'em straight to Heaven. An' then all the robin redbreasts i' th' wood were sorry 'bout it, an' they came an' covered 'em all over wi' beautiful red an' green leaves, 'cos God told the robins to bury 'em jest so, 'cos they wos good an' their ole' uncle wos bad, an' the robins did jest what God told 'em.' Her voice died away in a soft croodling whisper, and her eyelids drooped. 'Was that a nice story?' she asked.

'Very!' responded Lionel almost paternally, feeling quite old and wise, as he ventured now to put his own arm round her.

'I fink,' murmured Jessamine then – 'that 'oor bad ole Drojunwors 'as made me sleepy.'

And as a matter of fact, in a couple of minutes, the little maiden was fast asleep, her pretty mouth half open like a tiny rosebud, and the light rise and fall of her breathing suggesting the delicate palpitations of a dove's breast. Lionel sat very quiet, still encircling her with his arm, and looked dreamily about him. He studied the altar-screen immediately in front of him, regarding with somewhat of a gravely inquiring air the ancient, roughly carved oaken figures of the twelve apostles that partly formed it. He knew all about them of course – that they were originally common fishermen picked up on the shores of Galilee by Jesus the son of Joseph the carpenter, and that they went about with Him everywhere, while He preached the new strange Gospel of Love which seemed like madness to a world of contention, envy and malice. They were just poor ordinary men; not kings – not warriors – not nobly born – not distinguished for either learning or courage – and yet they had become far greater in history than any monarch that ever lived – they were evangelists, saints, nay almost secondary gods in the opinion of a section of 'semi-barbaric' mankind. It was very strange! – very strange indeed, thought Lionel as he gazed earnestly at their quaint wooden faces – and stranger still that a mere man who was a carpenter's son, should have made the larger and more civilised portion of humanity believe in Him as God, for more than eighteen hundred years! What had He done? Why, nothing – but good. What had He taught? Nothing – but purity and unselfishness. What was He? A determined reformer, who strove to upset the hard and fast laws of Jewish tradition, and unite all classes in one broad and holy creed of love to God and Brotherhood – a union of the Divine and Human which should ultimately lead to perfection. Even the various tutors who had taken their several turns at setting poor Lionel's little mind like a knife to the grindstone of learning, had been unable to say otherwise than that this Nazarene carpenter's son was good and wise and brave. In goodness none ever surpassed Him – that was certain. Socrates was wise and brave – but he was not actually good – many sins could be laid to his charge, and the same could be asserted of all the other famous moralists and philosophers who had essayed to teach the various successive generations of men. But against Christ, nothing could be said. True, He denounced the Jewish priesthood on the score that they were hypocrites; 'and surely' – thought Lionel with a prescience beyond his years, 'He would have to denounce the Christian priesthood, too, if it is true, as my father says, that they all preach what they don't believe, simply to gain a living.' He sighed – and his eyes wandered to the 'big lilies on th' Lord's table' with a wistful yearning. Those great white cups of fragrance! – with what sweet pride they stood up, each on its green stem, and silently breathed out praise to the Creator of their loveliness! 'Behold the lilies of the field! – they toil not, neither do they spin, and yet I say unto you that Solomon in all his glory was not arrayed like one of these.' How true that was! Put 'Solomon in all his glory' or any monarch that ever existed beside 'one of these' tall fair flowers, and he in his coronation-robes and crown, would seem but a mere doll-puppet decked out in tawdry tinsel. Lionel drew the little Jessamine closer to him as she slept, and sighed again – the unconscious sigh of a tired young thing overweighted with thought, and longing for rest and tenderness. The summer sunlight streamed down upon the two children with a broad beneficence, as though the love of Christ for the weak and helpless were mixed with the golden rays – as though the very silence and purity of the light expressed the Divine meaning – 'These "little ones" are Mine as the lilies are Mine! Suffer them to come to Me and forbid them not, for of such is the Kingdom of Heaven.' And as Lionel mused and dreamed, becoming gradually drowsy himself, the church-door swung softly open, and Reuben Dale, the verger, entered, with another and younger man, who carried a roll of music under his arm, and who immediately ascended alone to the organ-loft. Dale meanwhile paused, lifting his cap reverently, and looking about him in evident search for his little girl. Lionel beckoned to him from the pulpit-stairs, at the same time laying a finger on his lips to intimate that Jessamine was asleep. Honest Reuben advanced on tip-toe and surveyed the two small creatures encircled in one another's arms, with undisguised and good-natured admiration.

'Now that's jest prutty!' he murmured inaudibly to himself – 'An' as nat'ral as two young burrds! An' yon poor pale little lad looks a'most as if he was 'appy for once in's life!'

At that moment a solemn chord of sound stirred the air – the organist had commenced his daily practice, and was deftly unweaving the melodious intricacies of a stately fugue of Bach's, made doubly rich in tone by the grave pedal-bass with which it was sustained and accompanied. Lionel started – and Jessamine awoke. Rubbing her chubby little fists into her eyes, she sat up, yawned and stared – then smiled bewitchingly as she saw her father.

'We wos babes i' th' wood' – she explained sweetly – 'An' we wos waitin' fur the robins to come an' cover us up. Onny I specs they couldn't git froo th' windows to bring th' leaves.'

'I 'specs not indeed!' said Dale, the kind smile broadening on his mouth and lighting up his fine eyes – 'Now ye jest coom out o' that there poopit, ye little pixie – it's dinner-time, an' we'se goin' 'ome.'

Jessamine rose promptly and skipped down the pulpit-stairs, Lionel following her.

'Coom along wi' us,' – she said taking him affectionately by the arm – 'Ain't 'e a'-coomin', feyther? – 'e be a rare nice boy!'

'If s' be as 'e likes to coom, why sartinly an' welcome!' responded Reuben – 'But he's a little gemmun as 'as got a feyther an' mother o's own, an' mebbe they wants 'im.'

Lionel stood silent and inert. They were going away 'home' – this cheery verger and his pretty child – and the old creeping sense of oppression and loneliness stole over the boy's mind and chilled his heart. The music surging out from the organ-loft moved him strangely to thoughts hitherto unfamiliar, – and he thought he would stay alone in the church and listen, and try to understand the subtle meaning of such glorious, yet wordless eloquence. It seemed like angels singing – only there were no angels! – it made one fancy the gates of Heaven were open – only there was no Heaven! – it suggested God's great voice speaking tenderly – only there was no God! A deep sigh broke from him – and all unconsciously two big tears rose in his eyes, and splashed down wet and glistening on his little blue woollen vest. In a second the impulsive Jessamine had thrown her arms about him.

'O don't 'ee ky!' she crooned fondly in his ear – 'We'se both goin' 'ome wi' feyther, an' 'e'll be kind t' ye! An' when we've 'ad our dinner I'll show 'ee my dee ole 'oss! – *such* a nice ole 'oss 'e be!'

Despite himself, Lionel laughed, though his lips still trembled. Poor boy, he could hardly himself understand the cause of his own emotion – why his heart had given that sudden heave of pain – why the tears had come – or why he had felt so desolately, sorrowfully alone in a huge, cold, pitiless world – but he was grateful to Jessamine all the same for her sympathy. Reuben Dale meanwhile had been studying him gravely and curiously.

'Would 'ee reely like to coom an' take a snack wi' us, little zur?' he asked gently and with a certain deference – 'Ours is onny a poor cottage, ye know, an' sadly out o' repair – we'se 'ad no lord o' th' manor coom nigh us for many a year to look arter us an' see how we be a-farin' – none o' them fine folks cares for either our souls or bodies, purvidin' they gits their money out o' our labour an' worrit. All we 'as by way o' remembrance from 'em is a "love-letter" twice a year a-claimin' o' their rent – they never fails to send us that 'ffectionate message' – and his eyes twinkled humorously – 'but as fur puttin' a new fence or a new roof or makin' of us comfortabler like for our money, Lor' bless 'ee, they never thinks o't. But if ye'll take us as ye find us, ye'll be right welcome to coom on an' play wi' Jessamine a bit longer.'

'Thank you very much – I should dearly like to come' – said Lionel wistfully – 'You see I am all alone just now – my tutor went away this morning, and another tutor is coming tonight to take his place – but in the meantime there is nothing for me to do, as the plan of my studies is going to be changed – it is always being changed – and so I may as well be here as at home. I am giving myself a holiday today' – here he raised his eyes and looked Reuben Dale straight in the face – 'and I wish to tell you, Mr. Dale, that I am doing it without my father's knowledge or permission. I am so tired of books! – and I love to be out in the fresh air. Of course now you know this, you mayn't wish to have me, but then if you will please say so, I will go into the woods for the rest of the day, or stay by myself in the church. I should like to see more of the church – it interests me.'

Dale regarded the little fellow steadfastly, first in doubt and perplexity – then with a broadening smile.

'Tired o' books, be 'ee?' he queried – 'Well! – ye're young enough, sure-*ly*! An' books can wait awhile for ye. Reyther than go wanderin' i' th' woods by y'self, ye'd better coom along wi' me an' Jessamine – onny mind, ye must tell yer feyther where ye ha' been – ye must be sartin zure o' that!'

'Of course I'll tell him' – responded Lionel manfully – 'I always tell him everything, no matter how angry he is. You see he is very often angry, whatever I do or say – though he means it all for my good. He is a very good man – he has never done anything wrong in all his life.'

'Aye aye! Then he's jest a miracle!' said Reuben drily – 'Well now, little zur, 'fore we goes, I'll take ye round th' church – there ain't much to see, but what there is I know more about than any one else in Combmartin. Coom! – look at these 'ere altar-gates.'

He spoke in soft tones, and trod softly as befitted the sanctity of the place – and the two children followed him, hand in hand, as he approached the oaken screen and pointed out the twelve apostles carved upon it.

'Now do 'ee know, little zur,' said he, 'why this 'ere carvin' is at least two hunner' years old – an' likely more'n that?'

'No,' answered Lionel, squeezing Jessamine's little warm hand in his own, out of sheer comfort at feeling that he was not to be separated from her yet.

'Jest watch these 'ere gates as I pull 'em to an' fro,'[1] – continued Rueben – 'Do what ye will wi' 'em, they won't shut – see!' and he proved the fact beyond dispute – 'That shows they wos made 'fore the days o' Cromwell. For in they times all the gates o' th' altars was copied arter the pattern o' Scripture which sez – "An' the gates o' Heaven shall never be shut, either by day or by night." Then when Cromwell came an' broke up the statues, an' tore down the picters or whited them out wheresever they wos on th' walls, the altars was made different, wi' gates that shut an' locked – I s'pose 'e was that sing'ler afraid of idolatry that 'e thought the folks might go an' worship th' Communion cup on th' Lord's table. So now ye'll be able to tell when ye sees the inside of a church, whether the altar-gates is old or new, by this one thing – if they can't shut, they're 'fore Cromwell's day – if they can, they're wot's called modern gimcrackery. Now, see the roof!'

Lionel looked up, much impressed by the verger's learning.

'Folks 'as bin 'ere an' said quite wise-like – "O that roof's quite modern," – but 'tain't nuthin' o' th' sort. See them oak mouldings? – not one o' them's straight – not a line! They couldn't get 'em exact in them days – they wosn't clever enough. So they're all crooked, an' 'bout as old as th' altar-screen, mebbe older, for if ye stand 'ere jest where I be, ye'll see they all bend more one way than t'other, makin' the whole roof look lop-sided like, an' why's that d'ye think? Ye can't tell? Well, they'd a reason for what they did in them there old times, an' a sentiment too – an' they made the churches lean

1. The description of Combmartin Church in these pages is given as nearly as possible in the words of the late verger, one James Norman, who, all unconsciously, 'sat' to the author for the portrait of 'Reuben Dale.'

a bit to the side on which our Lord's head bent on the Cross when He said "It is finished!" Ye'll find nearly all th' old churches lean a bit that way – it's a sign of age, as well as a sign o' faith. Now look at these 'ere figures on the pews – ain't they all got their 'eds cut off?'

Lionel admitted that they had, with a grave little nod – Jessamine, who copied his every gesture for the moment, nodded too.

'That wos Cromwell's doin' ' – went on Reuben – ' 'E an' 'is men wos consumed-like wi' what they called the fury o' holiness, an' they thought all these figures wos false gods and symbols of idolatry, an' they jest cut their 'eds off – executed 'em as 'twere, like King Charles hisself. Now look up there,' – and he pointed to a narrow window on the left-hand side of the chancel – 'There's a prutty colour comin' through that bit o' glass! It's the only mossel o' real old stained glass i' th' church – an' it's a rare sight older than the church itself. D'ye know how to tell old stained glass from new? No? Well, I'll tell ye. When it's old it's very thick – an' if ye put your hand on its wrong side it's rough – very rough, jest as if it were covered wi' baked cinders – that's allus a sure an' sartin proof o' great age. Modern stained glass ye'll find a'most as smooth an' polished on its wrong side as on its right. Now, if ye coom into th' vestry I'll show ye the real old chest what wos used for Peter's pence when we wos under Papist rule.'

He led the way across the central aisle – Lionel followed, interested and curious, thinking meanwhile that this handsome white-haired verger could not exactly be called a stupid man, or even a 'semi-barbarian' – he was decidedly intelligent, and seemed to know something about the facts of history.

'There's an old door fur ye!' he said with almost an air of triumph as he paused on the vestry threshold and rapped his fingers lightly on the thick oak panels of the ancient portal – 'That's older than anything in the church – I shouldn't a bit wonder if it came out o' some sacred place o' Norman worship

– it looks like it. An' here's th' old key' – and he held up a quaint and heavy iron implement that looked more like a screw-driver with a cross handle than anything else – 'An' here's Peter's little money-box,' – showing a ponderous oak chest some five feet long and three feet high – 'That 'ud 'old a rare sight o' pennies, wouldn't it! Now don't you two chillern go a-tryin' to lift the lid, for it's mortal 'eavy, an' 'ud crush your little 'an's to pulp in a minnit. I'll let ye see the inside o't – there y'are!'

And with a powerful effort of his sinewy arms he threw it open, disclosing its black worm-eaten interior, with a few old bits of tarnished silver lying at the bottom, the fragments of a long disused Communion-service. Lionel and Jessamine peered down at these with immense inquisitiveness.

'Lor' bless me!' said Reuben then, laughing a little – 'There's a deal o' wot I calls silly faith left in some o' they good Papist folk still. There wos a nice ole leddy cam' 'ere last summer, an' she believed that Peter hisself cam' down from Heaven o' nights, an' tuk all the money offered 'im, specially pennies, fur they'se the coins chiefly mentioned i' th' Testament, an' she axed me to let 'er put a penny in – I s'pose she thought the saint might be in want o't. "For, my good man," sez she to me, "'ave you never 'eerd that St. Peter still visits th' world, an' when he cooms down 'ere, it may be he might need this penny o' mine to buy bread." "Do as ye like marm," sez I – "it don't make no difference to me I'm sure!" Well, she put the penny in, bless 'er 'art! – an' this Christmas past I wos a-cleanin' an' rubbin' up everythin' i' th' church, an' in dustin' out this 'ere box, there I saw that penny – St. Peter 'adn't come arter it! So *I* just tuk it!' and he chuckled softly – 'I tuk it an' giv' it to a poor old beggar-man outside the church-gate, so I played Peter fur once i' my life, an' not s' badly I 'ope, but wot I shall be furgiven!'

The smile deepened at the corners of his mouth and sparkled in his fine eyes as he shut the great coffer, and stood

66

up in all his manly height and breadth, surveying the two small creatures beside him.

'Well, do 'ee like th' old church, little zur?' he asked Lionel, whose face expressed an intense and melancholy gravity.

'Indeed I do!' answered the boy – 'But I think I like the music even better – listen! What is that?' And he held up one hand with a gesture of rapt attention.

'That's the hymn we allus sings on Harvest Thanksgiving Sunday – "Holy, Holy, Holy, Lord God Almighty, Early in the morning our song shall rise to Thee," ' – replied Reuben – 'It's a rare fine tune, an' fills th' heart as well as th' voice. Now little 'uns, coom 'ome to dinner!'

They passed out of the church into the warm sunlit air, fragrant with the scent of roses, sweet-briar and wild thyme, and drowsy with the hum of honey-seeking bees, Reuben Dale calling Lionel's attention as he went, to a great iron ring which was attached to the ancient door of entrance.

'Could 'ee tell me wot that ring's there for?' he demanded.

Lionel shook his head.

'Well, ye must ha' read in yer hist'ry books 'bout sanctuary privilege' – said Reuben – 'When any poor wretched thief or mis-rable sinner wos bein' a-hunted through the country by all the townspeople an' officers o' justice, 'e 'ad but to make straight for th' church-door an' ketch 'old of a ring like this an' 'e wos safe. It was "sanctuary" – an' no one dussn't lay a finger on 'im. 'Twos a rare Christian custom – it wos a'most as if 'e 'ad laid 'old of our dear Saviour's garment, an' found the mercy as wos never denied by Him to the weakest and wretchedest among us' – concluded Reuben piously, raising his cap as he spoke and looking up at the bright sky with a rapt expression, as though he saw an angel of protection there – 'An' that's the meaning o' th' iron ring.'

Lionel said nothing, but his thoughts were very busy. He was only a small boy, but his store of purely scientific information was great, and yet he knew not whether to pity or envy this 'semi-barbarian' for his simple beliefs. 'I should not like to tell him that all the clever men nowadays say that Christ is a myth' – he considered seriously, 'I am sure it would vex him.'

So he walked on soberly silent, holding the hand of the little Jessamine, who was equally mute, and Reuben led the way out of the churchyard, across the high road, and up a narrow street full of old-fashioned, gable-windowed, crookedly built houses, which at first sight appeared to lean over one another in a curiously lop-sided helpless way, as though lacking proper foundation and support. At one of these, standing by itself in a little patch of neatly trimmed garden, and covered with clusters of full-flowering jessamine and wistaria, Dale stopped, and rapped on the door with his knuckles. It was opened at once by a clean, mild-featured elderly dame in a particularly large white apron, who opened her lack-lustre yet kindly eyes in great astonishment at the sight of Lionel.

'Auntie Kate! Auntie Kate!' exclaimed Jessamine eagerly – 'This be a little gemmun boy – nice an' prutty 'e be! – we'se been playin' babes i' th' wood and Drojunwars all th' mornin', an' we'se goin' to 'ave our dinner an' see my ole 'oss arterwards!'

Auntie Kate did her best to understand this brilliant explanation on the part of her small niece, but failing to entirely grasp its meaning, looked to Reuben for further enlightenment.

'This is Master Valliscourt,' – said the verger then – 'The little son o' the gemmun wot 'as took the big 'ouse yonder for summer. He's bin fagged-like wi's lessons, an' 'e's just out on the truant as boys will be at times when they've got any boyhood in 'em; – giv' 'im a bit an' a sup wi' us, Kitty, an' 'e'll play a while longer wi' Jessamine 'fore 'e goes 'ome.'

Auntie Kate nodded and smiled – then in deference to 'Master Valliscourt,' curtseyed.

'Coom in, sir! – coom in, an' right welcome!' said she – 'Sit 'ee down, an' make 'eeself comfortable. Dinner's ready, an' there's naught to wait for but jest to let Reuben wash 'is 'ands an' ask a blessin'. Now my Jessamine girl, take off your bonnit an' sit down prutty!'

Jessamine obeyed, dragging off the becoming white sun-bonnet in such haste that she nearly tore one of her own brown curls away with it. Lionel uttered an exclamation of pain at the sight, and went to detach the rebellious tress from the string with which it had become knotted. He succeeded in his effort, and when the bonnet was fairly taken off, he thought the little maid looked prettier than ever, with her rough tumbled locks falling about her and her rosy face like a blossom in the midst of the chestnut tangle. Throwing off his own cap he sat down beside her at the table, which was covered with a coarse but clean cloth, and garnished with black-handled steel forks and spoons, and so waited patiently till Reuben came in from the washing of his hands, which he did very speedily. Auntie Kate then lifted off the fire a black pot, steaming with savoury odours, and poured out into a capacious blue dish a mixture of meat and vegetables – (more vegetables than meat) and finally set plates to match the dish. Reuben stood up and bowed his head reverently; 'For what we are going to receive, may the Lord make us truly thankful!' said he, and Jessamine's sweet little cooing voice answered 'Amen!' Whereupon they began the meal, which though so poor and plain, was good and wholesome. Auntie Kate was no mean cook, and she was famous in the village for a certain make of 'pear cordial,' a glass of which she poured out for Lionel, curtseying as she did so, and requesting him to taste it. He found it delicious; and he likewise discovered, to his own surprise, that he had an appetite. It was very remarkable, he thought, that Reuben Dale's frugal fare should have a better flavour than anything he had ever had at his own father's luxuriously appointed table. He did not realise that the respite

69

from study, the temporary liberty he was enjoying, and the romp with Jessamine, had all given room for his physical nature to breathe and expand; and a sense of the actual pleasure of life when lived healthily, had roused his exhausted faculties to new and delightful vigour. With this momentary development of natural youthful energy had come the appetite he wondered at, when the simplest food seemed exquisite, and Auntie Kate's 'pear cordial' suggested the ambrosial nectar quaffed by the gods of Olympus. The dinner over, Reuben Dale again stood up, and said 'For what we have received, may the Lord make us truly thankful!' and once more his little girl responded demurely 'Amen!' Then he proceeded to fill and smoke a pipe, before returning to the churchyard to complete the digging of 'Mother Twiley's' last resting-place, and Jessamine, still wearing the 'pinny' her aunt had tied round her while she ate her dinner, seized Lionel by the hand and dragged him off to the 'back yard' which was half garden, half shed, where Reuben kept his tools, and where a couple of smart bantams with their clucking little harem of prettily-feathered wives and favourites, strutted about behind a wire netting and imagined themselves to be the rulers of the planet.

'Coom an' see my ole 'oss!' said Jessamine excitedly – 'Such a good ole 'oss 'e be! 'Ere 'e is! – a-hidin' behin' th' wall! See 'im? O my bee–oo–ful ole 'oss!'

And she threw her arms round the neck of the quadruped in question, which was nothing else but a battered wooden toy that had evidently once been a gallant steed on 'rockers', but which now, without either mane, tail, or eyes and with three shaky legs and a stump of wood to support it, presented a very sorry spectacle indeed. But to Jessamine this 'ole 'oss' was apparently the flower of all creation, for she hugged it and kissed its pale nose, from which the paint had long since been washed off by wind and weather, with quite a passionate ardour.

'Oh my *dee* ole 'oss!' she murmured tenderly, patting its

hairless neck – 'Do 'ee know why I loves 'ee? 'Cos 'ee's poor an' ole, an' no one wants to ride 'ee now but Jessamine! Jessamine can git on 'ee's poor ole back without 'urtin' of 'ee, *good* ole 'oss! Kiss 'im, won't 'ee?' she added, turning to Lionel. '*Do* 'ee kiss 'im! – it makes 'im feel comfortabler now 'e's poor an' ole!'

Who could resist such an appeal! Who would refuse to embrace a superannuated wooden rocking-horse, described with so much sweetly pitiful fervour as 'poor an' ole,' and therefore in need of affectionate consolement! Not Lionel – despite the many learned books he had studied, he fully entered into the spirit of all this childish nonsense, and bending over the dilapidated toy, he kissed its wan nose with ardour in his turn.

'That's right!' cried Jessamine, clapping her hands delightedly – 'Now 'e feels 'appy! Now 'e'll give us a ride!'

And forthwith she clambered up on the gaunt, worn back of her beloved steed, showing a pair of little innocent-looking white legs as she did so, and jerked herself up and down to imitate a gallop.

'Ain't 'e goin' well!' she exclaimed breathlessly – her hair blowing in a golden-brown tangle behind her, and her cheeks becoming rosier than the rosiest apples with her exertions, while the laughter in her pretty eyes rivalled the brightness of the sunlight playing round her – 'Oh 'e be a rare nice ole 'oss! Now Lylie 'ee must git up an' 'ave a ride!'

Lionel started at the sound of his mother's pet name for him – then he remembered he had told it to Jessamine, and smiled as he thought how sweet it sounded from her lips. And he answered gently:

'I'm afraid I'm too big dear! Your horse couldn't carry me – I might hurt him.'

'Oh no 'ee won't 'urt' im!' declared Jessamine, springing lightly to the ground – 'Try an' git on 'im! – I'se sure 'ee'll be good t'ye!'

Thus adjured, Lionel threw a leg across the passive toy, and pretended to ride at full gallop as Jessamine had done, much to the little maiden's delight. She danced about and shrieked with ecstasy, till the bantams behind the wire netting evidently thought the end of the world had come, for they ran to and fro, clucking in the wildest excitement, no doubt imploring their special deities to protect them from the terrible human thing that showed its white legs and danced in the sun almost as if it had as a good a right to live as a well-bred fowl. Reuben Dale, hearing the uproar and having finished his pipe, came out to see what was going on, and laughed almost as much as the children did, now and then playfully urging the wooden steed to a wilder exhibition of its 'mettle' by a stentorian 'Gee-up Dobbin!' which rather added to the general hilarity of the scene. When the game was quite over, and Lionel flushed and full of merriment, resigned the 'ole 'oss' to Jessamine, who at once offered it a handful of hay and whispered tender nothings in its broken ear, the verger said:

'Now, my little zur, I'm a-goin' back to my work i' th' churchyard, for I must finish Mother Twiley's bed 'fore nightfall. Ye'll find me there if ye'se want me. If s'be ye care to stay on wi' Jessamine a bit, ye can – she's a lonesome little un' since 'er mother went to God – and mebbe you're lonesome too – a little play'll do neither o' ye 'arm, an' Auntie Kate's i' th' house all day, an' she'll look arter ye. But ye mustn't be away too long from yer feyther an' mother – ye must git 'ome 'fore the sun sets, my lad – promise me that!'

'Yes, Mr. Dale, I promise: – and thank you!' responded Lionel eagerly – 'I've had such a happy time! – you don't know how happy! I may come again some day and see you and Jessamine, mayn't I?'

'Why sartin zure ye may!' said Reuben heartily. 'Purvidin' they makes no objections at your own 'ome, little zur – ye must make that clear an' straight fust.'

'Oh yes! – of course!' murmured the boy – but a shadow

clouded his hitherto bright face. He knew well enough that if his father were asked about it, not only the acquaintance, but also the very sight of the kindly verger and his pretty child would be altogether forbidden him. However he said nothing of this, and Reuben after a few more cheery words, strode off to the resumption of his labours. With his departure a silence fell on the two little creatures left alone together; the excitement engendered by the 'ole 'oss' had its reaction, and Jessamine grew serious, even sad.

'I *fink* I wants my sun-bonnet' – she remarked in an injured tone – 'My facey burns.'

Lionel ran into the house at once, and obtained the desired head-gear from Auntie Kate, whereupon Miss Jessamine adjusted it sideways, and peered at him in a sudden fit of shyness.

' 'Specs 'eed better go 'ome now' – she said severely – 'You'se tired of me an' my ole 'oss – I sees you'se tired!'

'Tired, Jessamine! Indeed I'm not tired! – I'll play with you ever so long! – as long as you like. What shall we do now?'

'Nuffink!' replied the little lady, putting the string of her bonnet in her mouth, which was a favourite habit of hers, and still regarding him with an odd mixture of coyness and affection; – then, with sudden and almost defiant energy she added – 'I *knows* you'se tired of me, Lylie!'

'Now Jessamine, *dear*!' expostulated Lionel, with quite a lover-like ardour, as he saw that the tiny maiden was inclined to be petulant – 'Come and sit under that beautiful big apple-tree!'

'*My* big apple-tree!' put in Jessamine, with an air of grave correction – 'That's *my* tree, Lylie!'

'That's why it's such a nice one,' – declared Lionel gallantly, taking her little hand in his own – 'Come along and let us sit there, and you'll tell me another story, or I'll tell you one. You know I'm going away very soon, and perhaps I shall never see you again.'

He sighed quite unconsciously as he said this, and Jessamine looked up at him with eyes that were angelically lovely in their momentary gravity.

'Will 'ee be sorry?' she asked.

'Very sorry!' he answered – 'Dreadfully sorry!'

Jessamine's doubtful humour passed at this assurance, and she allowed him to lead her unresistingly to the big apple-tree which was the chief ornament of Reuben Dale's back garden – *her* tree, against whose gnarled trunk a rough wooden seat was set for shelter and repose.

'I'll be sorry too!' she confessed – ' 'Specs I'll ky when you'se gone, Lylie!'

There was something touching in this remark, or they found it so – and a deep silence followed. They sat down side by side, under the spreading apple-boughs laden with ruddy fruit that shone with a bright polish in the hot glow of the afternoon sun, and holding each other's hands, were very quiet, while round and round them flew butterflies and bees, all intent on business or love-making; and a linnet who had just cooled his throat at the bantams' water-trough, alighted on an opposite twig and essayed a soft *cadenza*. There were a thousand sweet suggestions in the warm air – too subtle for the young things who sat so demurely together hand in hand, to perceive or comprehend; – the beautiful things of God and Nature, which wordlessly teach the eternal though unheeded lesson, that happiness and good are the chief designs and ultimate ends of all creation – and that only Man's perverted will, working for solely selfish purposes, makes havoc of all that should be pure and fair. Yet even children have certain meditative moments, when they are vaguely conscious of some great Benefice ruling their destinies – and some of them have been known at a very early age to express the wonder as to why God should be so good, and their own parents so bad.

'What will 'ee do when 'ee gits 'ome?' inquired Jessamine presently – 'Will 'ee ky?'

Lionel smiled rather bitterly. 'No, Jessamine, it would never do for me to cry' – he said – 'I'm too big.'

'Too big!' she echoed – 'You'se onny a *weeny* bit bigger 'n me! An' I'se little.'

'Yes, but you're a girl' – said Lionel – 'Girls can cry if they like – but boys mustn't. I do cry sometimes though, when I'm all by myself.'

'I seed 'ee ky today,' observed Jessamine gravely – 'I' th' church – jest 'fore we come 'ome to dinner. What did 'ee ky then for?'

'It was the music I think' – answered Lionel with a far-away look in his deep-set eyes – 'I'm very fond of music, but it always seems sad to me. My mother sings beautifully, but somehow I can never bear to hear her singing – it makes me feel so lonely.'

Jessamine gazed at him sympathetically. He was surely a very strange and funny boy to feel 'lonely' because his mother sang. Presently she essayed another topic.

'I knows th' big 'ouse where 'ee lives' – she announced – 'There's a 'ole in th' 'edge, an' I can creep froo – into th' big garden! I'll coom an' see 'oor muzzer!'

This statement of her intentions rather startled Lionel. He looked earnestly into her sweet blue eyes.

'You mustn't do that, Jessamine dear!' he said sadly – 'You would get scolded I'm afraid. My mother would not scold you – but I expect my father would.'

Jessamine put a finger into her mouth and sucked it solemnly for a minute – then spoke with slightly offended dignity.

' 'Oor feyther is a bad ole man!' she said calmly – 'Onny a bad ole man would scold me, 'cos I allus tries to be good. *My* feyther never scolds me, nor my ole 'oss neither.'

Lionel was silent. She cuddled closer to him.

'I *muss* see 'ee 'gain, Lylie!' she crooned, plaintively – 'Doesn't 'ee want to see *me* no more?'

Her baby voice was inexpressibly sweet as she pathetically

asked this question, and Lionel, unaccustomed as he was to any kind of affectionate demonstration, felt a strange beating of his young heart as he looked down at the small child-face that was turned so wistfully towards him.

'Yes, dear, dear little Jessamine, I do want to see you again, and I *will* see you! – I'll come as often as ever I can!' and daring thoughts of shirking his tasks and eluding Professor Cadman-Gore's eye, flitted through his brain, in the same way as the scaling of walls and the ascending of fortified towers have suggested themselves to more mature adventurers as worthy deeds to be accomplished in the pursuit of the fair. 'I'll come and play with you whenever I can get away from my lessons – I promise!'

' 'Iss – do!' said Jessamine, coaxingly – ' 'Cos I likes 'ee, Lylie – I doesn't like any other boys 'ere, – they'se all oogly. You'se prutty – an' – an' I *fink* I'se prutty too! – sometimes!'

Oh small witch! That 'sometimes' was the very essence of delicate coquetry, and accompanied, as it was, by a little smile and arch upward twinkle of the blue eyes, was irresistibly fascinating. Lionel felt, though he knew not why, that this little damsel must be kissed – kissing seemed imperative – yet how was it to be done?

'You are very pretty, Jessamine dear,' he said, with a winsome mingling of boldness and timidity, 'You are just as pretty as a flower!' Jessamine nodded in serene self-complacency, while her youthful admirer peered at her close-curved red lips much as a bird might look at a ripe cherry, and was silent so long that at last she gazed straight up into his eyes, the heavenly blue of her own shining with a beautiful wonder.

'What's 'ee thinkin' 'bout, Lylie?' she asked.

'You, Jessamine!' the boy answered tenderly, 'I was thinking about you – and the flowers.'

And bending down his curly head he kissed her – and the little maiden, nestling closer, kissed him innocently back. Overhead the fragrant apple-branches swung their sweet burden of ruddy fruit and green leaf to and fro with a soft rustle in the summer breeze, and the linnet who lived in the topmost bough carolled his unpretentious little song, and the fairness of the world as God made it, seemed to surround with an enchanted atmosphere the two children who, drawn thus together by the bond of a summer-day's comradeship and affection, were happy as they never would be again. For the world as God made it, is one thing – but the world as Man mars it, is another – and life for all the little feet that are to trudge wearily after us in the hard paths which we in our arrogant egoist-generation, have strewn for them so thick with stones and thorns, offers such a bitter and cruel prospect, that it is almost a matter of thanksgiving when the great Angel of Death, moved perchance by a vast pity, gently releases some of the fairest and tenderest of our children from our merciless clutches, and restores them to that Divine Master and Lover of pure souls, who said – 'Take heed that ye despise not one of these little ones, for I say unto you that in heaven their angels do always behold the face of My Father.'

CHAPTER 6

THE sun was well-nigh upon sinking when Lionel, walking slowly and with reluctant steps, returned to his home. As he approached the house he saw his mother at the entrance gate, apparently waiting for him. Looking at her from a little distance he thought how very beautiful she was – more beautiful than ever he had quite realised her to be. Her rich hair shone in the brilliant sun-glow with wonderful golden glints and ripples, and her eyes were lustrous with a dreamy tenderness, which softened and grew deeper as he came up to where she stood. She stretched out her hand to him – a delicate little hand, white as a white rose-petal, and sparkling with the rare diamond rings that adorned the taper fingers.

'Why, Lylie, where have you been all day?' she asked gently – 'Your father's very angry; he has been searching for you everywhere and making all sorts of inquiries in the village. Some one has told him that you were at the inn this morning, seeing Mr. Montrose off by the early coach, and that afterwards you ran away with some common boys to play hide-and-seek; is that true?'

'No, mother, it isn't true' – the boy answered quietly – 'Not altogether. I did go to see Mr. Montrose off by coach – that's correct enough; but I never ran away to play hide-and-seek with any common boys – if I had wanted to, they wouldn't have had me, I daresay. I don't play games; you know that; there's no one to play them with me. I fancied I would like to stroll about all by myself – I was tired of books – so I went into the old church-yard and found the sexton there at work digging a grave, and he is such a nice old man that I stayed there and talked to him. Then his little girl came to bring him some coffee, and I went with her inside the church, and Mr.

Dale – that's the sexton – showed me all over it and explained all the old historical bits – and then he asked me to his house to dinner. I thought it very kind of him, and I was pleased to go. I've just come from there, and that's the truth, mother, exactly as it happened.'

Mrs. Valliscourt slipped her arm round his neck. She was smiling to herself rather oddly.

'Poor Lylie!' she said caressingly – 'So you were really tired, were you, and determined to have a real good time for once in your own way? Well, I don't blame you! I should do the same if I were in your place. But your father's in a great rage – he wanted you to be here to receive Professor Cadman-Gore — '

'But, mother, he's not expected till ten o'clock tonight!' exclaimed Lionel.

'I know – that's the time we thought he was coming. But he's got rheumatism, or lumbago, or something of that sort and decided at the last minute that it would be best for him to arrive in daytime and avoid the night air. So he took an earlier train from London and caught the afternoon coach from Ilfracombe, and he's here – in fact he has been here nearly two hours shut up with your father in his room.'

Lionel was silent for a minute or two – then he asked:

'What's he like, mother? Have you seen him?'

Mrs. Valliscourt laughed a little.

'Oh yes, I've seen him. He was formally introduced to me on arrival. What's he like? – well, I really don't know what he's like – he's a cross between a very old baboon and a camel – rather a difficult animal to define!'

Her flashing smile irradiated her whole countenance with a gleam of scorn as well as amusement – Lionel however looked pained and puzzled. She gave him a little side-glance of infinite compassion, and suddenly drawing his head against her breast, kissed him. Any caress or sign of affection from her was so rare a thing that the sensitive little lad actually trembled and grew pale with the emotion it excited in him – it left him almost breathless, and too astonished to speak.

'I mean, dear,' she continued, still keeping her arm about him – 'that he is just like all those wonderfully learned old men who have ceased to care about anything but themselves and books – they are never by any chance handsome, you know. He's very clever though – your father thinks him a prodigy, and so, I believe, do all the Oxford and Cambridge dons – and now he's here you'll have to make the best of him, Lylie!'

'Yes, mother.' The answer came faintly, and with a smothered sigh. Then – after a brief pause – Lionel took the white hand that rested against his neck, kissed it, and gently put it aside.

'I think I'd better go straight in to father at once and tell him where I've been' – he said bravely: 'Then it's over and done with. No matter how angry he is, he can't kill me – and if he could, it would be worse for him than for me!'

With this unanswerable piece of cynical logic and a wistful parting smile, he quickened his steps almost to a run, and went into the house. Mrs. Valliscourt stood still on the garden-path, idly ruffling the petals of a rose in her waistband, and watching the thin, delicate figure of her little son till he disappeared; – then she turned away across the lawn, moving vaguely, and unseeing where she went, for her eyes were heavy and blind with a sudden rush of tears.

Meanwhile Lionel reached his father's room and boldly knocked at the door.

'Come in!' cried the harsh voice he knew so well, whereupon he entered.

'Father — ' he began.

Mr. Valliscourt rose in his chair, a stiff bristling-haired spectre of wrath.

'So, sir!' he said. 'You have come home at last! Where

have you been since the early hours of the morning? And what business had you to leave this house at all without my permission?'

Lionel looked at him full in the eyes with a curious coldness. He was conscious of a strange feeling of contempt, for this red-faced man, spluttering with excitement, whose age, experience, education and muscular strength could help him to no better thing than the bullying of a small boy. It might be a wicked feeling – considering that the red-faced man was his own father – but wicked or no, it existed. And so without any soft or weak emotion of regret or penitence, he replied indifferently:

'I was tired. I wanted to be in the open air and rest.'

'Rest!' Mr. Valliscourt's eyes protruded, and he put his hand to his shirt-collar in evident doubt as to whether his throatful of bubbling rage might not burst that carefully-starched halter – 'Rest! Good heavens, what should a lazy young animal like you want with rest! You talk as if you were an over-worked bank clerk begging for an out-of-time holiday! You are always resting; – while Mr. Montrose was here you never did anything – your idleness was a positive disgrace. Do you think I am going to waste my money on giving you the best tuition that can possibly be procured, to be rewarded in this ungrateful manner – this shameful, abominable manner —'

'Is *he* the best tuition?' demanded Lionel suddenly, pointing to a second personage in the room whom he had noted at once on entering, and whom he recognised to be the 'cross between a baboon and camel' his mother had described – a forbidding-looking old man with a singularly long pallid face and sharply angular shoulders, who sat stiffly upright in a chair, regarding him through a pair of very round spectacles. Mr. Valliscourt stared, rendered almost speechless by the levity of the question.

81

'How dare you, sir! – How dare you make such an unbecoming observation!' he gasped. 'What – *what* do you mean, sir?'

'I only asked,' returned Lionel composedly; 'You said you were throwing your money away on the best tuition, and I asked if *he were* the best tuition' – again pointing to the round spectacles opposite – 'I didn't say he wasn't – I suppose he is. But I'm afraid he'll find me rather a trouble.'

'I'm afraid he will indeed!' said Mr. Valliscourt with cutting severity – then – turning to the gaunt individual in the chair beside him, he continued – 'I much regret, Professor, that you should have such an unpromising introduction to your pupil. My son – this *is* my son – has been sadly demoralised by the influence of the young man Montrose, but I trust not so completely as to be beyond your remedy.'

Professor Cadman-Gore, the dark-lantern of learning and obscure glory of University *poseurs*, slowly raised his bony shoulders up to his long ears, and as slowly settled them in their place again, this being his own peculiar adaptation of the easy foreign shrug – then, smiling a wide and joyless smile, he replied in measured monotonous accents:

'I trust not – I trust not.' And he readjusted his spectacles. 'But I will not disguise from you – or from myself – that this is a bad beginning – very bad!'

'Why?' asked Lionel quickly – 'Why is it a bad beginning to rest when you are very tired and want it? Some people believe that even God rested on the seventh day of creation, that's why we keep Sunday still, in spite of its being only an idea and a fable. I've taken a holiday today, and I'm sure I shall do my lessons all the better for it. I've been talking to the sexton of Combmartin Church, and I've had dinner with him – he's a very nice old man, and very clever too.'

'Clever! The sexton of Combmartin!' echoed Mr. Valliscourt with a loud fierce laugh – 'Dear me! What next shall we be told, I wonder! Nice associates you pick up for yourself, sir, after all the labour and expense of your training! I might as well have kept my money!'

'Why not begin to keep it now, father?' suggested Lionel rather wistfully, the pallor deepening on his delicate small face – 'It's no use spending it on me – I know it isn't. I'm tired out – perhaps I'm ill too – I don't know quite what's the matter with me, but I'm sure I'm not like other boys. I can see that for myself, and it worries me. If you'd let me rest a little, I might get better.'

'Desire for rest,' remarked Professor Cadman-Gore with a sardonic grin, 'appears to be the leading characteristic of this young gentleman's disposition.'

'Incorrigible idleness, you mean!' snapped out Mr. Valliscourt, 'United, as I now discover, to my amazement and regret, with an insolence of temper which is new to me. I must apologise to you Professor, for my son's extraordinary conduct on this occasion. Starvation and solitude will probably bring him to his senses in time for the morning's studies. I may as well explain to you that I never use corporal punishment in the training of my son – I employ the mortification of appetite as the more natural means of discipline. That, and solitary confinement seem to me the best modes of procedure for the coercion of a refractory and obstinate nature.' The Professor bowed, and linking his leathery hands together caused the knuckles to emit a sharp sound like the cracking of bad walnuts. 'Lionel,' continued Mr. Valliscourt – 'Come with me!'

Lionel paused a moment, looking at his new tutor with an odd fascination.

'Goodnight, Professor!' he said at last – 'Tomorrow I shall ask you a great many questions.'

'Indeed!' returned the Professor grimly – 'I have no doubt I shall be able to answer them!'

'*Will* you come, sir!' roared Mr. Valliscourt.

Lionel obeyed, and followed his father passively upstairs

to his own little bedroom, where Mr. Valliscourt took the matches carefully away, and shut down and fastened the window. This done, he turned to the boy and said:

'Now here you stay till tomorrow morning – you understand? You will have time to think over your wicked disobedience of today – the anxiety you have caused me, and the trouble – the disgraceful exhibition you have made of yourself to the Professor – and I hope you will have the grace to feel sorry. And if you cry or make a row up here – '

'Why do you talk like that, father?' queried Lionel, simply, – 'You know well enough that I never make a row.'

Mr. Valliscourt stopped, looking at him. For a moment he was embarrassed by the direct truth of the remark – for he did know – Lionel never showed any sign of petulance or fury. The boy meanwhile put a chair at the window facing the sunset, and sat down.

'What made you run away today?' asked his father, after a brief pause.

'I have told you already' – responded Lionel, somewhat wearily – 'I was tired.'

'Tired of what?'

'Of books and everything in them. They are very puzzling, you know – no two writers agree on any one point – no two histories are alike – it is all quarrel, quarrel, muddle, muddle. And what's the good of it all? You die, and you forget everything you ever knew. So your trouble's wasted and your knowledge useless.'

'Little fool! You have first to live before you die, and knowledge of books is necessary to life' – said Valliscourt harshly.

'You think so? Ah! – well, I haven't quite made up my mind about that' – answered the boy with a quaintly reflective air – 'I must consider it carefully before I decide. Goodnight, father.'

Mr. Valliscourt gave no reply. Striding out of the room he banged the door angrily, and locked it behind him. Lionel remained by the window, looking straight into the golden glare of the west. He was not at all unhappy – he had had one day of joyous and ever-memorable freedom – and that this lonely room should be the end of it did not seem to him much of a hardship. He was not afraid of either solitude or darkness – it was better to be alone thus, than to have to endure the presence of the gaunt and unwholesome looking object downstairs, who was reputed by a certain 'set' to be one of the wisest men in the world. A pity that wisdom made a person so ugly! – thought Lionel, as he recalled one by one the Professor's unattractive lineaments. What lantern jaws he had! – what cold, cruel little ferret eyes! – what an unkind slit for a mouth! – and how different was his crafty, artificially-composed demeanour to the open and sincere bearing of Reuben Dale.

'Reuben Dale could teach me a lot, I know,' – mused the boy – 'He doesn't read Greek or Latin I suppose – but I'm sure he could help me to find out something about life, and that's what I want. I want to understand what it means – life – and death.'

He lifted his eyes to the radiant sky, and saw two long shafts of luminous amber spring outward and upward from the sinking sun like great golden leaves, between which the orb of light blossomed red like a fiery rose in heaven.

'I wish there were angels, *really*,' – he said half aloud – 'One would almost think there must be, and that all that splendid colour was put into the sky just to show us what their beautiful wings are like. Little Jessamine Dale believes in angels – I should like to believe in them too – if I could.'

His gaze wandered slowly down from the sunset, to the shrubs and trees of the garden below him, and presently he saw among the darkening shadows two figures moving leisurely up and down. One was his mother – he recognised her by the white serge dress she wore – the other was a man whose personality he was not at first quite sure of, but whom he afterwards made out to be Sir Charles Lascelles.

'I suppose he's come to dinner,' – thought Lionel – 'I remember now – Mr. Montrose mentioned that he was staying quite near here at Watermouth Castle. I wonder why I don't like him?'

He considered this for some time without clearing up the point satisfactorily – then, before it grew quite dark, he took out Montrose's copy of Homer from under his blue jersey vest where he had secreted it, out of his father's sight, and put it carefully by in readiness to post to its rightful owner next day, smiling a little to himself as he thought of Jessamine's odd pronunciation of the 'Drojunwors'. This done, he resumed his seat by the window, and watched the skies and the landscape till both grew dark, and the stars began to twinkle out dimly in the hazy purple distance. His little mind was always restless, and actively evolving ideas – and though his immediate reflections dwelt for the most part on the pretty face and winsome ways of Jessamine Dale, they now and then took a more serious turn and strove to make something out of what appeared to him an ever-deepening problem and puzzle – namely – why should some people believe in a God, and others not? And why should so many of those who professed belief, live their lives in direct opposition to the very creed they assumed to follow? There must be adequate cause for all these phases of human nature. Did the world make itself? – or did it owe its origin to a reasoning and reasonable Creator? – and not only the world, but all the vast universe – the thousands of millions of glorious and perfect star-systems which like flowers in a garden, bloomed in the pure ether – what was the object of their existence, if any, and why was it decided that they should exist, and WHO so decided it? Deep in the child's brain the eternal question burned – the eternal defiance which always asserts itself when there is neither faith nor hope – the suicidal scorn which disdains and upbraids a

Force that can give no reason for its actions, and which re-
fuses to act in blind obedience to the cross-currents of a fate
that leads to Nothingness. 'If you can offer me no worthy
explanation of my existence, and I can supply none for
myself' – says the tortured and suffering soul – 'then not all
the elements shall hinder me from putting an end to that
existence if I please. This much I can do – if you give me no
satisfactory motive for my hold on life I can cease to live, and
thus are your arguments confuted and your surface-knowledge
made vain.'

The seed of this spiritual rebellion was in Lionel's mind
though he knew it not – it had been sown there by others,
and was not of his own planting, nor the natural out-put of his
being. His unceasing query as to the 'why' of things, had
never been answered by the majestic reason known to those
whose faith is raised upon high pinnacles of thought and
aspiration – and who hold it as a truth that their lives are lived
by God's will and ordinance in the school of temporal begin-
nings as a preparation for eternal fulfilment. This supreme
support and hope had not been given to the boy's frail life
to raise it like a drooping flower from the dust of material
forms and facts – he had been carefully instructed in all the
necessary science for becoming a man of hard calculation and
cool business-aptitude – but his imagination had been promptly
checked – he had never even been taught a prayer, although
he had been told that there *were* people who prayed – in
churches and elsewhere. When he propounded the usual
'why?' he was informed that the fashion of praying was the
remains of old superstition, followed now out of mere ordinary
usage, because the 'masses' of the people were not yet sufficiently educated to do entirely without the observances to
which they had for so many centuries been accustomed – but
that it was only a matter of foolish habit. And then his teachers
pointed out to him that the laws of the universe being inflexible, it was ridiculous to suppose that prayer could alter them,

or that the deaf, dumb, blind forces of nature could possibly note a human being's trouble, or listen to a human being's complaint, much less accede to a human being's request – for human beings, compared with the extent of Creation generally, were no more than motes in a sunbeam, or ants on an ant-hill. Hearing this, and quickly grasping the idea of man's infinite littleness, Lionel at once set about asking the cause of man's evident arrogance. If he were indeed so minute a portion of the creative plan, and so valueless to its progress, why was he so concerned about himself? If he were but a mote or an ant, what did it matter whether he were learned or ignorant? – and did it not seem somewhat of a cruel jest to fill him with such pride, aspiration and endeavour, when according to scientific fact, he was but a grain of worthless and perishable dust? To all these serious questions, the small searcher after truth never got any satisfactory replies. Montrose indeed had told him with much emphasis, that man possessed an immortal Soul – a conscious individual, progressive Self, which could not die – which took part in all the designs of God, and which, filled with the divine breath of inspiration and desire of holiness, was borne on through infinite phases of wisdom, love and glory for ever and ever, always increasing in beauty, strength, love, and purity. Such a destiny, thought Lionel, would have made one's present life worth living, if true. But then, according to modern scientists, it wasn't true, and Montrose was a poor 'semi-barbarian' who still believed in God, and who had got his dismissal from his post as tutor, chiefly on that account.

'I wonder,' mused Lionel, 'what it is that makes him believe? It can't be stupidity, for he is very clever and kind and good. I wish I knew exactly why he thinks there is a God – and Reuben Dale too – he has just the same idea – only when I ask, no one seems able to give me any clear explanation of what they feel.'

Darker and darker grew the evening shadows – but still he

sat at the window, solemnly considering the deep problems of life and time, and never thought of going to bed. Soon a misty white glory arose out of the gathering blackness, the moon, pallid yet brilliant, lifted her strangly sorrowful face over the plumy tree-tops and cast a silvery reflection on the grass below. It was a mournful, almost spectral night – a faint bluish haze of heat hung in the stirless air – dew sparkled thickly in patches upon the distant fields with a smooth sheen as of shining swamps, or suddenly risen pools – and in the furthest thickets of the garden, a belated nightingale who ought by laws ornithological, to have hushed his voice more than a month since, sang drowsily and as if in a dream, without passion, yet with something of pain. Lionel heard the faint, throbbing notes afar off, and would have liked to open the window to listen more attentively, but as his father had shut and fastened it, he decided to leave it so; – and presently, watching what with the moon and the lengthening ghostly shadows, and thinking and wondering, he fell fast asleep in his chair, his head leaning against the wall. For a long time he remained thus, dreaming odd disjointed dreams, in which the various facts he had learned of history got mixed up with little Jessamine Dale and the 'ole 'oss', the latter object becoming in his visions suddenly endowed with life, and worthy to bear a Coeur de Lion to the field of battle. All at once he was startled into broad wakefulness by a voice calling softly, yet clearly:

'Lionel! Lionel!'

He jumped up, and to his amazement saw the stalwart figure of Sir Charles Lascelles comfortably perched on a branch of the big elm-tree that grew just outside his window. The baronet had a package in his hand, and with it made signs of peremptory yet mysterious meaning. Not knowing what to think of this strange proceeding, the boy noiselessly unfastened and raised the window.

'Oh, there you are, little chappie!' said Sir Charles, showing his white teeth in a pleasant smile, and swinging himself further along the branch in order to approach the window more nearly – 'Look here – your mother sends you this – catch!' and he dexterously threw the packet he held straight into the room, where it fell on the floor – 'Sandwiches, cake and pears, my boy! – eat 'em all and go to bed. The old man's been boasting of his cleverness in starving you – he's shut himself up now with that blessed ass of a professor, so he won't know anything about it – and your mother says you're to eat every morsel, to please her. Ta-ta!'

Lionel thrust his little pale eager face out of the window.

'Oh, please, Sir Charles!' he called faintly after the retreating baronet. Lascelles looked back.

'Well?'

'Give mother my love – my dear love – and thank her for me.'

Sir Charles turned his face upward in the silver shimmer of the moon. There was a curious expression upon it, of shame, mingled with tenderness and remorse.

'All right, my boy – I will! Good-night!'

'Good-night!' responded Lionel. And he stood at the open window for a minute or two, inhaling the night air, fragrant with the odour of flowers and the breath of the sea – and mar-velling at the athletic adroitness with which Sir Charles, who generally 'posed' as a languid and lazy man of fashion, slipped along the elm-branch, swung himself downward by both hands, dropped stealthily to the ground, and disappeared. No burglar could have been more secret or swift in his actions, or more sudden in his coming and going. Alone once more, the boy shut and fastened the window again with soft pre-caution – then he felt along the floor for his mother's package. He soon found and opened it – there were plenty of good things inside – and, spreading his repast on the window-sill with the moonbeams for light, he was surprised to find himself really hungry. He very seldom felt any decided relish for food

– and he did not realise that his one day's free 'outing' in the Devonshire air, was the cause of his healthy appetite. To-morrow, and the next day, and the next, when he should resume his poring over books, and his patient if weary researches into 'works of reference', he would find the old indifference, lassitude and nausea upon him again – the lack of energy which deprived him not only of appetite, but even of joy in exercise – which made a walk fatiguing, and a run impossible. But now his little moonlit feast seemed delightful – and he was quite happy when, having finished the surreptitious meal, he undressed and slipped into bed. He was soon asleep, and the white moonrays streaming in at the uncurtained window fell slantwise on his small classic face and ruffled curly hair. Some pleasing vision sweetened his rest, for he smiled – that divine half-wondering, half-solemn smile which is never seen save on the lips of sleeping children, and the newly dead.

CHAPTER 7

THE next morning Professor Cadman-Gore sat awaiting his pupil in what was called the 'school-room' – the bare, uncurtained apartment in which Lionel had been puzzling over his books when Willie Montrose had called him out from study to the fresh air and the salty scent of the sea. It was an old-fashioned room, with a very low ceiling which was crossed and re-crossed by stout oak rafters, after the style common to Henry the Eighth's period, and had evidently been formerly used as a storeroom both for linen and provisions, for all round the walls there were large oaken cupboards holding many broad shelves, and here and there among the rafters were yet to be seen great iron hooks, strong enough to support a pendent dried haunch of venison, or possibly a whole stag, antlers included. The Professor, being tall, found some of these hooks considerably in his way – he had already knocked his bald pate rather smartly against one of them, which he had instantly turned upon, as though it were a sentient enemy, and endeavoured to wrench out of position. But the tough rusted iron resisted all his efforts, and he had only scratched his hands and wasted his time without gaining his object. Somewhat irritated at this trifling annoyance – trifles always irritated him – he seated himself in the most comfortable chair available, and looked out of the window which was a quaint and pretty lattice-work casement opening on two sides, in the French fashion. The lovely scent of sweet-briar assailed his nose and offended it – the gardener was cutting the grass, and the dewy smell suggested hay-fever at once to his mind.

'What a fool I was to consent to come to this out-of-the-way place!' he muttered ill-temperedly; 'Considering the distance from town, and the discomfort of the surroundings,

I ought to ask double fees. The man Valliscourt is a prig – thinks he knows something, and doesn't know anything – his wife is good-looking and has all the impudent self-assurance common to women of her type – and the boy seems to be a little puny-faced ass. Talk of the quiet of the country! – ugh! – I was wakened up this morning by the incessant crowing of a cock – what people buy such brutes of birds for, I don't know – then a wretched cow began lowing – and as for the twittering of the birds, why it's a positive pandemonium – worse than a dozen knife-grinders at work. I'll have all those creepers cut away that are climbing round my bedroom window – they harbour insects as well as birds, and the sooner I get rid of both nuisances the better.'

He blew his long nose violently, with a startlingly-tinted silk handkerchief of mingled red and yellow hues – and the idea of hay-fever again recurring to him, he shut the window with a bang. Then he unfolded a large sheet of paper which Mr. Valliscourt had given him the previous night, and on which was written out in neatest copperplate the 'schedule' or plan of study Lionel had been following for the past six months. Over this document he knitted his yellow forehead, grinned and frowned – as he read on, he blinked, sucked his tongue, and smacked his lips, and twisted himself about in so many fidgety ways that he became a perfectly appalling spectacle of ugliness, and in his absorbed condition of mind was not aware that the door of the room had quietly opened, and as quietly closed again, and that Lionel stood confronting him, with a calmly speculative and critical stare. Two or three minutes passed silently in this way – then Lionel spoke.

'Good morning, Professor!'

The Professor started, and rapidly disentangled his long legs from the uncouth knot in which he had gathered them over the edge of the chair he occupied – put down the 'plan' – adjusted his round spectacles, and surveyed his pupil.

'Good-morning, sir!' he responded drily – 'I trust you have slept off your temper, and are prepared for work?'

'I haven't slept off my temper' – said Lionel quietly, 'because I had no temper to sleep off. Father knew that as well as I did. It's always silly, I think, to accuse somebody else of being in a temper when you're in one yourself. But that's all over now – that was yesterday – this is today, and I am quite prepared for work.'

'Glad to hear it!' and Professor Cadman-Gore smiled his usual pallid smile – 'Have you had your breakfast?'

'Yes.'

'And have you "rested" sufficiently?' demanded the Professor with sarcastic emphasis.

'I don't know – I don't think so,' – the boy answered slowly – 'I often feel I should like to go to sleep for days and days.'

'Really!' and a prolonged sniff indicated the learned tutor's deep disdain – 'Possibly you are of the hybernating species?'

'Possibly!' responded Lionel, with cynical calm. 'A hybernating animal is a creature that goes to sleep all the winter. I shouldn't mind that at all – it would take off a lot of trouble from one's life. Don't *you* ever feel tired?'

'Physically speaking, I am occasionally fatigued;' – said the Professor, eyeing him severely – 'Particularly when I have to train and instruct foolish and refractory natures. Mentally, I am never weary. And now, if you have no further observations of immediate importance to make, perhaps you will condescend to commence the morning's work.'

Lionel smiled, and tossed back his curly hair with a pretty, half-proud half-careless gesture.

'Oh, I see what you are like now!' he said – 'You are what they call of a satirical turn of mind – and it is part of your particular kind of fun to ask me if I will "condescend" to work, when you know a boy like me can't have his own way in anything, and has to do what he's told. I know what is

94

meant by satire – Juvenal was a satirist. I made an essay on him once – he began as a poet, but he got tired of writing beautiful things for people who wouldn't or couldn't understand them – so he turned round and ridiculed everybody. He got exiled to Egypt for making fun of one of the Emperor Hadrian's favourites – and they say he died out there of vexation and weariness, but I think it was more from old age than anything else, because he lived till he was eighty, and that made him older, I daresay, than even you are now.'

The Professor's nose reddened visibly with irritation.

'Older? – I should think so indeed! – very much older!' he snapped out – 'It will be a very long time before *I* am eighty.'

'Will it?' queried Lionel simply – 'Well, one can only go by looks, you know, and you look old, and I'm not at all clever at guessing people's ages. Will you ask me some questions now, or will you teach me something I am very anxious to know, first?'

The Professor glanced him over from head to foot with grim disparagement.

'I think,' he said, 'it is my turn to examine you, if you have quite done examining me. It is necessary for me to know how far you have actually progressed in your studies, before I set you fresh tasks. Referring to the plan so admirably drawn up by your father, it seems you should know something of Greek and Latin – you should also be considerably advanced in mathematics, and you should be fairly strong in history. Stand where you are, please – put your hands behind your back, in case you should be inclined to twiddle your fingers – I hate all nervous movements' – the learned gentleman was apparently unaware of his own capacity for the 'fidgets' – 'and when you give an answer, look me straight in the face. I have my own special method of examination, which you will have to accustom yourself to.'

'Oh yes!' replied Lionel cheerfully – 'Every tutor has his

own special method, and no two methods are alike. It is difficult at first to understand them all – but I always try to do my best.'

The Professor made no response, but set to his work of catechising in terrible earnest, and before an hour had passed, was fairly astonished at the precocity, intelligence, and acute perception of his pupil. The child of ten had learnt more facts of science and history, than he, in his time, had known when he was twenty. He concealed his surprise however, under the cover of inflexible austerity, and the more apt to comprehension Lionel proved himself to be, the more the eminent pedagogue's professional interest became excited, and the more he determined to work such promising material hard. This is often the fate of brilliant and intelligent children – the more quickly they learn, the more cruelly they are 'crammed', till both heart and brain give way under the unnatural effort and forced impetus, and disaster follows disaster, ending in the wreck of the whole intellectual and physical organisation. Happy, in these days of vaunted progress, is the dull heavy boy who cannot learn – who tumbles asleep over his books, and gets a caning, which is far better than a 'cramming'; – who is 'plucked' in his exams and dubbed 'dunce' for his pains; – the chances are ten to one, that though he be put to scorn by the showy college pupil loaded with honours, he will, in the long run, prove the better, aye, and the cleverer man of the two. The young truant who Mother Nature coaxes out into the woods and fields when he should be at his books – who laughs with a naughty recklessness at the gods of Greece, and has an innate comic sense of the uselessness of learning dead languages which he is never to speak, is probably the very destined man who, in time of battle, will prove himself a hero of the first rank, or who, planted solitary in an unexplored country, will become one of the leading pioneers of modern progress and discovery. Over-study is fatal to originality of character; and both clearness of brain and strength of physique are denied to the victims of 'cram'.

Professor Cadman-Gore was an advocate of 'cramming'; – he was esteemed in many quarters as the best 'coach' of the day, and he apparently considered a young human brain as a sort of expanding bag or hold-all, to be filled with various bulky articles of knowledge, useful or otherwise, till it showed signs of bursting – then it was to be promptly strapped together, locked and labelled – 'Registered Through Passenger for Life'. If the lock broke and the whole bag gave way, why then so much the worse for the bag – it was proved to be of bad material, and its bursting was not the Professor's fault. His filmy eyes began to sparkle with a dull glitter, and his yellow cheeks reddened at their jaw-bone summits, as he took note of the methodical precision and swiftness with which the young Lionel assorted his 'facts' in sequence and order – of the instantaneous, hawk-like fashion in which the boy's bright brain pounced, as it were, on a difficult proposition in Euclid and solved it without difficulty – and a lurking sense of the *unnaturalness* of such over-rapid perception and analysis in a child of ten, intruded itself now and then on his consciousness – for among other matters, the Professor had studied medicine. Yet his knowledge of the science was so slight that he was not without fears of instant death whenever he had a mild attack of dyspepsia, and he considered himself seriously wounded if he managed to run a pin into his finger. Nevertheless, a few trite medical statements did occur to his memory as he put Lionel through his paces – recognised axioms concerning over-precocity of brain and acute cerebral excitement of nerve-centres – but he did not permit himself to dwell upon them. On the contrary, he worked the boy as he would have worked a muscular young fellow of eighteen or twenty, and Lionel himself showed no signs of weariness, owing to the complete rest and release from tension he had enjoyed the previous day. Things that often presented themselves to him as a useless 'muddle', now suddenly seemed quite simple and clear; and he was sensible of a curious, almost feverish desire to astonish his new tutor by his quickness. An inward precipitate volition hurried him on, causing him to spring at difficulties and overcome them – and he gave all his answers with a fluency and rapidity that was bewildering even to himself. At the conclusion of the morning's work, Professor Cadman-Gore reluctantly stated that he was 'fairly well satisfied' wtih the results of his preliminary interrogations.

'You will, however,' he continued – 'need to apply yourself more closely to study than you have hitherto done, if you are to be at all a credit to *me*. I must tell you I very seldom undertake the tuition of a boy of your age – it is too much trouble, and too little honour – but as you have gone on so far, and your father seems anxious about you, I shall do my best to put you well ahead. I am now going to write down the course of reading you will undertake this afternoon, and the dozen "subjects" you will prepare for tomorrow – I shall expect you not only to be word-perfect, but sense-perfect. I want absolute and distinct comprehension – not parrot-like repetition merely.'

'I am only having *holiday* tasks'; – put in Lionel with a wistful air – 'Do you know that?'

'Of course I know it. Such work as you are given now is comparatively light, to what you will be able to perform when the regular term begins. You are preparing for a public school – Winchester?'

'No – I don't think so – I should like to – but – '

'H'm – h'm! – Now let me think!' And twitching his forehead and mouth in his usual nervous fashion, the Professor began to scribble his list of 'themes', while Lionel stood quietly beside him watching the great bony fingers that guided the pen.

'When you have done that, may I ask you the thing I want so much to know?' he inquired.

The Professor looked up with some curiosity. He was inclined to negative the proposition, but the boy's aptitude and intelligence, combined with his obedience and gentleness, had, to a very great degree, mollified the chronic state of irritation in which he, as a sort of modern Diogenes, was wont to exist – so after a pause, during which he went on writing, he replied –

'You may, certainly. Is it a matter of importance?'

'I think so!' and the boy's eyes darkened and grew dreamy – 'It seems so to me, at any rate. I am very anxious about it.'

Professor Cadman-Gore laid down his pen, and leaning back in his chair, widened his thin lips into what he meant to be an encouraging smile.

'Well, speak out!' he said – 'What is it?'

Lionel came close to him, and looked earnestly in his face.

'You see, you are very clever'; – he observed with deferential gentleness – 'Cleverer than anybody in all England, some people say. Well, then, you must have found out all about it, and you can explain what has been puzzling me for a long long time. What I want to know is this – Where is the Atom?'

The Professor gave a violent start – almost a jump – and stared.

'Where is the Atom?' he repeated – 'What nonsense are you talking? What do you mean?'

'It's not nonsense,' – declared Lionel with patient firmness – 'It can't be nonsense – because it is the cause of everything we know. We are alive, aren't we? – you and I and millions of people, and we're all in this world together. But books tell you that this world is only a very little planet, one of the smallest in the sky – and there are thousands and thousands, and millions and millions of other planets ever so much larger, some of which we cannot see, even with the longest and strongest telescope. Then, look at our sun! – we should not be able to live without it – but there are millions of other suns and systems – all separate universes. Now if all these

99

things are atoms, and are designed by an Atom – where is it? – that wonderful little First Atom which, without knowing in the least what it was about, and with nobody to guide it, and having no reason, judgment, sight or sense of its own, produced such beautiful creations? And then, if you are able to tell me where it is, will you also tell me where it came from?'

The Professor's eyes rolled wildly in his head, and he glared at the composed little figure and wistful earnest face of his pupil with something of dismay as well as annoyance.

'You see,' continued the boy anxiously – 'I should not have mentioned it to you, unless I had heard that you were so wise. I've been waiting for a very wise man to talk to about it, because it's been on my mind a long time. The tutor I had who is just gone, Mr. Montrose, had quite different ideas to those of all the scientists – he believed in a God, like all the uneducated, ignorant people. But before Mr. Montrose came I had a very clever tutor, a Mr. Skeet – he was a Positivist, he said, and a great friend of a person named Frederic Harrison, and he told me all about the Atom – and he explained to me that it was a fortuitous combination of such things that made universes. And it puzzled me very much, because I thought there must be a beginning even to these atoms, and I could not imagine how an Atom could think out a plan by itself, and create worlds with people bigger than itself on them. But he was a very funny man – Mr. Skeet, I mean – he used to say that nothing was everything, and everything was nothing. He said this so often, and laughed so much over it, that I was afraid he was going quite mad, so I used to avoid the subject altogether. Now you have come, I am sure you can make it clear to me so that I shall understand, properly, because it *is* very interesting, don't you think, to know exactly where the Atom is, and what it's doing?'

Slowly, and with an uncomfortable sense of bafflement, Professor Cadman-Gore rallied his scattered forces.

'You ask to know what no one knows;' – he said harshly –

'That there is a First Cause of things is evident – but where it is, and where it came from, is an unfathomable mystery. It is, in all probability, now absorbed in its own extended forces – all we know is, that it works, or *has* worked; and that we see its results in the universe around us.'

Lionel's face darkened with disappointment.

'You call it a First Cause;' – he said – 'And are you really quite sure that First Cause is an Atom?'

'No one can be sure of anything in such matters;' answered the Professor, wrinkling his brows – 'We can only form a guess, from what we are enabled to discover in natural science.'

A strange smile, half disdain, half sorrowful flashed in the boy's eyes.

'Oh then, you only "guess" at the Atom, as other people "guess" at a God!' he said – 'No one is sure about anything! Well, I think it is very silly to settle upon an Atom as the cause of anything. It seems to me much more natural and likely that it should be a Person. A Person with brain and thought and feeling and memory. In the works of nature there is no Atom which thinks out a universe for itself – if there were it would rule us all – '

But here the Professor rose up in all his strength, and swung a heavy battering-ram of explicit fact against the child's argument.

'And as a matter of positive truth and certainty, atoms *do* rule us!' – he interrupted with some excitement – 'The atoms of disease which breed death – the atmospheric atoms which work storm and earthquake – the atoms which penetrate the brain-cells, and produce thought – the atoms moving in a state of transition which cause change, both in the development of worlds and the progress of man – good heavens! – I could go on quoting hundreds of instances which prove beyond a doubt that we are entirely governed by the movement and conglomeration of atoms – but you are too young to understand – you could never grasp the advanced scientific doctrines of the day – it is ridiculous to discuss them with a boy like you!'

'I don't think it is ridiculous' – said Lionel placidly – 'because you see, I am rather an unhappy sort of boy. I think a good deal. If I were happy, I might not think; Mr. Montrose says there are lots of boys who never think at all, and that they get on much better than I do. But when one can't help thinking, what is one to do? Oh dear!' and he heaved a profound sigh – 'I did hope you would be able to clear up all my difficulties for me!'

The Professor rubbed his great hands together, cracked his knuckles and coughed awkwardly, but, was otherwise silent.

'You know,' went on Lionel, pathetically – 'it doesn't make you care very much about living, if you feel there's no good in it, and that you are only the smallest possible fraction of the results of an Atom, which didn't care and didn't know what it was about, when it started making things. I should be ever so much happier if I thought it were a Person who knew what He was doing. *We* are supposed to know what we are doing, even in very small trifles, and if we *don't* know, we are considered quite silly and useless. So it does seem rather funny to me, that we should decide that all the beautiful work of the universe is done by a thing that hasn't any notion what it is about. It would be much easier to understand, I think, if the scientific people could agree that the First Cause was a Person, who knew.'

Still the Professor was silent.

'A Person who knew,' continued the boy thoughtfully – 'would have ideas; and if He were a good Person, they would all be grand and beautiful ideas. And if He were an eternal Person, He would be eternally designing new and still more wonderful things, so we should not be surprised at knowing He had made millions and millions of stars and universes.

And if He were good Himself, He would never quite destroy anything that had good in it – He would be kind too, and He would always be improving and helping on everything He had made. Because as a Person, he would have feeling; – and when people got into trouble, or sickness, or poverty, He would comfort them somehow. *We* might not see how He did it, but He would be sure to manage it. He could not help being sorry for sorrow, if He were a good Person. Yes, the more I think of it the more likely it seems to me; – beautiful flowers and beautiful colours in the sky, and music – these things make the idea of a Person much pleasanter and more natural to me than an Atom.'

'An Atom may be a Person, or a Person an Atom,' said the Professor, beguiled into involuntarily argument, by the weird sagaciousness and old-mannish air of the little lad who still stood confidently close to his knee, looking frankly up into his hard furrowed face, and who at this observation, laughed softly.

'That sounds like Mr. Skeet, who said everything was nothing and nothing was everything!' he remarked; – 'But I don't think it could be so, you know! You can't make anything of an Atom; – you couldn't say it thinks, or sees. It would have to think and see, to arrange colours perfectly, and it would have to hear, in order to make harmonies. I've gone over all this ever so many times in my own mind, and this is how it seems to me. I believe – I do really believe, with all the wonderful discoveries we are making we shall find out the Atom to be a Person after all! And that He knows exactly what He's doing and what *we're* doing! What a good thing that will be, won't it? Because then we can some day ask Him to explain all that we don't understand. Of course we might ask the Atom, but I don't see how it could be expected to answer, as it is only supposed to be just working with no object in particular.'

The Professor felt an odd chill as of cold water running down his back at the strange arguments of this child, who he began to consider 'uncanny'. The suggestion that it would be 'a good thing' if the scientific Atom were discovered to be a Person, had something in it of positive terror; and the learned Cadman-Gore was disagreeably conscious that for him and his particular 'set', such a discovery would be anything but pleasant. Uncomfortable thoughts occurred to him – he knew not why – of the time when he, dry-souled man of dogmatic theory though he now was, had been a small inquisitive boy himself – and when he had recognised the very Person Lionel dimly imagined – the pure, fearless, grand image of God in Christ, to whom at his mother's knee he had daily and nightly prayed – but against whose divine faith and noble teaching, he, led away by plausible modern sophistries, now turned with a mockery and sarcasm exceeding the bitterness of any old-world Pharisee. For he was one of that new and 'select' band of men and women, who, enjoying the singular liberties and privileges of the Christian creed, are nevertheless unwearying in their attempts to destroy it; and who scruple not to stone the God-Founder, and crucify him afresh, with an ingratitude as monstrous as it is suicidal. Women especially, who, but for Christianity, would still be in the low place of bondage and humiliation formerly assigned to them in the barbaric periods, are most of all to be reproached for their wicked and wanton attacks upon their great Emancipator, who pitied and pardoned their weaknesses as they had never been pitied or pardoned before. And was not the Professor himself thinking seriously of espousing one such Christ-scorning female, with short hair and spectacles, who had taken high honours at Girton, and who was eminently fitted to become the mother of a brood of atheists, who, like human cormorants, would be prepared to swallow benefits, and deny the Benefactor? Such disjointed reflections as these chased one another through the eminent pundit's mind and ruffled his scholarly equanimity – he almost felt as if he would like to shake the boy who stood there, calmly propounding puzzles which could never be solved.

'You have talked quite enough on this subject,' he said roughly – 'and if you were to ask me questions for a year, I could tell you no more than science teaches. All religions are fables and impostures – the universe is not, and could never be, the work of a Person or persons. The ignorant may build themselves up a God if they choose – *we* know better. All creation, as you have already been told, is the result of a fortuitous concurrence of atoms – but where the first atom is, or where any of the atoms came from, is beyond human ingenuity to discover. We know nothing of the reasons why we live.'

Lionel's face grew very pale.

'Then life is a very cruel thing, and not worth having!' – he said – 'It is wicked indeed that people should be born at all, if no good is to come of it. If there's no reason for anything, and no future object for anybody, I don't see why we should take the trouble to live. It's all a mistake and a muddle; and a very stupid business, I think.'

The Professor rose from his chair, and stretching his long legs at ease, smiled a capacious smile.

'What *you* think is of no import;' – he observed grandiloquently – 'We are here – and being here, we must make the best of our time.'

'But what *you* think is of no import either;' returned Lionel simply – 'The Atom doesn't care any more about you than it does about me. It's all the same, you see. You are clever and I am stupid – and you are clever I suppose, because you like to please people by your cleverness – now I should never care about pleasing people – I would rather please the Atom if it could be pleased, because it is Everything, people included. But it can't be pleased, because it is blind and deaf and senseless – it just goes on twirling, and doesn't know anything even about itself. And whatever best we make of our time, it's no use, because we die, and there's an end. Will you like to die?'

The Professor felt himself becoming impatient and irascible.

'Certainly not! No sane man likes to die. I intend to live as long as possible.'

'Do you really? Just fancy!' and Lionel's eyes grew large with genuine astonishment – 'Now how different that is to me! – I would much rather die than live to be as old and wise as you are!'

'Do you mean to be insolent, sir?' demanded the Professor, growing suddenly livid with anger.

'Insolent? Oh dear no! – indeed no!' exclaimed the boy quickly – 'Did I say anything rude? If I did, I am sorry! Please excuse me – I meant no harm? Only I do think it seems dreadful to look forward to so many long, long years of work and trouble and worry, all for nothing – and that is why I would not like myself to live to be very old. Are you going out in the garden? – here is your hat – and your stick:' and he handed these articles with a pretty grace to the irritated pundit, who glowered down upon him, uncertain what to do or say – 'There are lots of beautiful roses growing wild – you will find them near the hedge that makes the boundary of the grounds – any quantity of them. Do you know I'm very glad the Atom managed to make roses as well as human beings!'

Professor Cadman-Gore clapped his hat well down on his bald head, and fixed his severe eye on the small philosopher.

'Read that chapter I have marked for you in Caesar's Commentaries,' – he said gruffly – 'It will steady your ideas. You are inclined to be flighty and fantastic – now let me tell you once and for all, I don't like fads or fancies of any kind. Stick to facts – master *them* thoroughly – and it is possible I may make something of you. But let me hear no more nonsense about atoms and universes – *this* world is your business – and beyond this world you have *no* business!'

With that, he strode out – and Lionel, left alone, sank wearily into his vacated chair.

'It's very funny – but I've always noticed people get angry over what they can't understand!' he mused – 'And they won't listen to any suggestions, or try to learn, either. The Professor knows as well as I do, that there is a Cause for everything – only he won't take the trouble to reason it out as to whether it's an Atom or a Person. He's got a theory, and nothing will alter it. Now Reuben Dale believes in a Person – I wish I could see Reuben again, and ask him one or two questions.'

He sighed profoundly – and feeling the air of the room oppressive, he opened the lattice-window and looked out. It was high noontide; the sun was hot on the flower-beds – the geraniums flared scarlet fire – the petunias drooped fainting on their slim velvety stalks – only the great sunflowers lifted themselves proudly aloft to give their bright deity golden stare for stare – the birds, overcome by the heat, were mute, and in hiding under cool bunches of green leaves. On a side-path shaded by elm-trees, Lionel presently caught sight of the Professor walking up and down with his father, in earnest conversation, and as he watched them he smiled, a weird little smile.

'They are talking about me, I daresay!' he reflected – 'The Professor is very likely telling my father what a curious boy I am to ask questions about the Atom, or anything that has to do with the reasons of our being alive – and perhaps they will get into an argument on the subject themselves. Well! – it may be curious, and no doubt it's very troublesome of me to want to know why we live, and what's the good of it – but I can't help it. I do want to know – I don't see how anyone can help wanting to know – and I think it would be much more interesting and useful to study and find out these things, than to learn Greek and Latin.'

Then, being a very docile little creature, and wishful to

please even the grim old tutor now placed in authority over him, he moved away from the window, seated himself at the big table-desk, and opened Caesar's Commentaries at the marked chapter, which he read and meditated upon with grave patience till called to dinner.

CHAPTER 8

THE days now went on monotonously in a dull and regular
routine of study. To learn, was made the chief object of
Lionel's existence – and the only relaxation and exercise he
had was a solemn walk with the Professor along the dusty
high-road every afternoon. That distinguished pedagogue did
not care for woods and fields – he detested the sea – and the
mere suggestion of a scramble on the shingly beach of Combmartin would have filled him with horror. Nothing would ever
have induced him to enter a boat, or climb a hill – and his
sole idea of a walk was a silent tramping 'constitutional' along
a straight road in the glare of the sun. He took large strides,
and sometimes Lionel's little legs had difficulty in keeping up
with him – while as to conversation, there was none. The
Professor's knowledge of things in general was derived from
books – Lionel's ideas were the instinctive efforts of natural
aspiration – and the two did not commingle. Moreover, if his
young pupil showed the slightest tendency to discuss any
more difficult and vexatious problems concerning life, death
or eternity, the learned Cadman-Gore invariably became
abstracted and lost, in the profoundest of profound reveries,
and twitched his brows and sucked his tongue, and made
himself look altogether so alarmingly ugly, that he successfully
warned off and kept at a distance all undue familiarity and
confidence. Lionel however had by this time discovered the
wisdom of holding his peace – he shut up his thoughts within
himself, though at times they seemed to be getting too much
for him, and often kept him awake at night, giving him an odd
burning pain and heaviness in his head. And the old lassitude
and languor from which he was wont to suffer had returned
upon him with redoubled intensity, while the vivacity and

brightness with which he had astonished his tutor on the first morning of his examination by that eminent 'coach', had completely vanished. His progress now was slow – and the Professor declared him to be a 'disappointment'.

As a matter of fact, the poor little lad found his tasks growing heavier and heavier each day – each day he felt less inclined to work – and the mass of information he was expected to master grew daily more and more of a confusion and muddle. At times, too, he was conscious of a very dreadful sensation which frightened him – a kind of wild desire to scream aloud, jump from the open window, or do something that would be wholly unlike himself, and inexplicable to reason. At such moments, he would clench his small hot hands hard, bite his lips, and apply himself more assiduously to his lessons than ever, though the nervous terror of his own feelings often became so strong as to make him tremble and turn cold from head to foot. But he never complained; – and save that to a close observer his eyes appeared heavier, and his mouth more set in the pained line of hard self-control, his looks never betrayed him.

One fine day fortune favoured him with a brief respite from toil, and an equally brief glimpse of happiness. His father and Professor Cadman-Gore suddenly decided to go on an excursion together to Lynmouth and Lynton, called by some enthusiasts 'the Switzerland of England', though this term is sadly misplaced. The snowy peaks and glittering glaciers of the Alps cannot be brought into a moment's comparison with the up-hill and down-dale prettinesses of Lynton, which is surpassed even in its own neighbourhood by the romantic loveliness of the ideal village known as Clovelly, while its over-abundance of foliage makes it somewhat gloomy and depressing to the spirits, though it offers a beautiful picture to the eyes. The Professor however was anxious to test its claim to be a 'Switzerland' personally – and Mr. Valliscourt who prided himself on having 'read up' the local centres of interest, resolved to accompany him as 'guide, philosopher and friend'. They arranged therefore to go by coach, remain the night at the 'Castle Hotel', which commands the finest view of the whole valley of Lynmouth, and return to Combmartin the following morning. Lionel was left well supplied with work, and was likewise severely warned not to go farther astray than the garden surrounding the house – Mrs. Valliscourt having driven early into Ilfracombe to spend the day with some of her London friends, who were staying there, and she was not expected back till late in the evening.

'You will have the house to yourself – and this will be an excellent test of your obedience;' said Mr. Valliscourt, as when he was prepared to start on his pleasure trip, he stood for a moment frowning heavily down on his small pale son – 'I suppose you know what is meant by a word of honour?'

'I suppose so!' – answered the boy, with a slight, weary smile.

'Then you will give me your word of honour not to leave these grounds' – went on his father. 'This is a large garden – quite sufficient for you to take exercise in – and if you conscientiously study the subjects selected for you, you will not have much time to waste in rambling. No more running about Combmartin like one of the common village boys, and scraping acquaintance with sextons – do you hear?'

'I hear!' said Lionel.

'And you promise not to leave the grounds?'

'On my word of honour!' and Lionel again smiled, this time rather disdainfully.

'He has a fairly good idea of the obligations of duty'; – put in Professor Cadman-Gore, gathering together his shaggy brows – 'I consider that to be his strongest point.'

Lionel said nothing. He had nothing to say; if he had uttered what was in his mind, it would neither have been understood nor attended to. Grown men have little patience with the troubles of a child, though such troubles may be as deep and acute as any that are endured by the world-worn veteran. Nay, possibly more so – for sorrow is a strange and cruel thing to the very young, but to the old it has become a familiar comrade, whose visitations being of almost daily occurrence, are met with comparative equanimity.

When at last his father and the Professor had fairly gone, and he had actually seen them pass the house on the top of the coach, being driven away from Combmartin, the boy was sensible of a sudden great relief, as though a burden had been lifted from his heart and brain. He leaned out of the school-room window inhaling the fresh air, and his weirdly thoughtful little visage looked, for a few moments almost as young as Nature meant it to be. He was sorry his mother was not at home – he would have liked to run downstairs and find her, and kiss that beautiful face which had softened into such unusual tenderness for him when he had returned home from his stolen holiday. Perhaps she might come back early from Ilfracombe – he hoped she would! If her friends did not detain her as long as she expected, it was possible he might see her and talk to her before he went to bed. A vaguely comforting idea stole into his mind that she – his own dear, beautiful mother – loved him after all, though it was difficult to believe it! Very difficult – because she hardly ever spoke to him, never expressed a wish to have him with her, and truly appeared to take little or no interest in his existence. And yet, . . . Lionel could not forget the sweet look of her eyes, or the sudden kiss she had given him on that memorable afternoon of his truant wanderings, now nearly a fortnight ago. He sighed; – a whole fortnight had passed! – and he had had no cessation from work, no respite from the crushing society of Professor Cadman-Gore, till today! Today was a real godsend and must be made the best of, he said to himself, as he gazed wistfully at the lovely undulations of wood and hill and meadow, all bathed in the amber haze of summer warmth which softened every feature of the landscape, and made it look more dream-like than real. The sun was so bright and the grass so green, that he presently decided to go and study his lessons in the garden – and selecting a couple of books from the pile which the Professor had left in order on the school-room table, he put them under his arm and went out. He drew a long breath of pleasure when he found himself in the side-path running parallel to the boundary hedge where the roses grew – their exquisite fresh faces, pink, white and red, seemed to smile at him as he approached, and the odour exhaled from their dewy centres suggested happy fancies to his mind. Strolling up and down in delightful solitude, he forgot all about his books, or rather thought of them just sufficiently to relieve himself from the burden of them, by putting the two he carried aside on a garden-seat, there to await his pleasure. And presently he threw himself down full length on a sloping bank of mossy turf warmed by the sun, and folding his arms behind him, let his head rest upon them while he gazed straight up into the infinite reaches of the glorious blue sky. There sailed a straight bit of fleecy cloud – here flew a swift-winged swallow – and immediately above him, quivering aloft among the sunbeams like a jewel suspended in mid-heaven, carolled a lark, with all that tender joyousness which has inspired a poet to write of it thus:

'From out the roseate cloud, athwart the blue,
    I hear thee sound anew
That song of thine a-shimmering down the sky,
    And daisies, touched thereby,
Look up to thee in tears which men mistake for dew.

I see thee clip the air, and rush and reel,
    As if excess of zeal
Had giddied thee in thy chromatic joys; –
    And overhead dost poise
With outstretched wings of love, that bless while they
    appeal.

Thou hast within thy throat a peal of bells,
  Dear dainty fare-thee-wells! –
And like a flame dost leap from cloud to cloud: –
  Is't this that makes thee proud?
Or is't that nest of thine, deep-hidden in the dells?

Whate'er they meaning be, or vaunt or prayer,
  I know thy home is there:
And when I hear thee trill, as now thou dost,
  I take the world on trust,
And with the world thyself, thou foeman of despair!'

The leafy branches of the trees were delicately outlined in air as with an artist's careful pencil – no breeze stirred them – and the exceeding loveliness of nature, without man's cruelty to mar it, gave the boy's heart a strange pang. If the jarring voice of his father had suddenly startled the silence, something dark, yet undefinable, would, he knew, have blotted out all the beauty of the scene. A thrush alighted near him, and ruffling out its speckled breast, looked at him inquisitively with its bright round black eyes – there was no discordant element in the bird's intrusion, but there would have been in his father's presence. He tried in his own odd way to analyse this feeling, and started on his usual themes of troubled thought; – did his father really love him ? – did his mother? – was there any good in his loving them? – and what was to come of it all? All at once as he lay musing, some one called him by his pet-name —

'Lylie! Lylie!'

He jumped to his feet, and looked about everywhere, but could see nobody.

'Ly-lee-e!'

This time the prolonged sound seemed to come from the boundary hedge against which the roses grew, and where there was a mixture of many other blossoms, such as are found growing in wild and varied beauty all along the lanes in Devonshire. He went close up to it, and glancing eagerly hither and thither, suddenly perceived a little rosy face in an aureole of gold-brown curls, cautiously peeping through a tangle of white jessamine and green briony and smiling at him with a half-bold, half-frightened glee.

''Ullo, Lylie! I sees 'ee!' and the face pushed itself further through the veiling screen of foliage and flowers – ''Ullo, Lylie!'

'Why, Jessamine dear!' exclaimed Lionel, flushing with pleasure at the sight of the winsome little maid he had hardly ever expected to meet again – 'How did you manage to come? How did you find your way?'

Little Miss Dale did not reply immediately. Looking round in every direction, she demanded:

'Can't I git right froo? – an' see 'oor muzzer?'

Lionel thought rapidly of the chances of detection – of the gardener who might be acting as a spy on him by his father's orders – of the other servants who might also be on the watch – and though not at all afraid for himself, he had no desire to get Reuben Dale and his little girl into trouble. So he went down on his knees in front of the jessamine flowers and Jessamine herself, and drawing her little baby face to his own, kissed it with a simple boyish tenderness that was very sweet and commendable.

'My mother isn't here today' – he said softly for fear of being overheard – 'She's gone to Ilfracombe to see some friends and won't be back till evening. My father and my tutor are away too, and I'm all alone. I've promised not to leave the garden, or I should have come to see you, Jessamine. How's Mr. Dale?'

'My feyther's quite well' – responded Jessamine, with some solemnity; 'He's diggin' another grave, – a weeny weeny grave – for a little tiny baby. Oh, such a prutty grave it be!'

She sighed – put her finger in her mouth, and raised her blue eyes pensively, like a dreaming angel.

'How's 'ee feelin', Lylie?' she asked presently with sudden concern – ' 'E looks white – very white, Lylie, 'ee looks – like my muzzer when she went to Heaven.'

Lionel smiled.

'I've been doing a lot of lessons, Jessamine,' he replied – 'That's what it is, I suppose. Books make you get pale, I think. *You* never read books, do you?'

Jessamine shook her head.

'I can't read' – she confessed – 'I can spell – an' I know my fairy-book. Auntie Kate tells me my fairy-book, an' God's Book. That's all.'

Fairy-book and God's Book! Here began and ended Jessamine's literary knowledge. Lionel smiled, as the grim picture of Professor Cadman-Gore involuntarily presented itself, and he thought of the disdain in which that erudite individual held both fairy-books, God's Book, and the very idea of God, that wished-for 'Person' who Lionel would have preferred to recognise rather than the scientific Atom. And kneeling on the warm grass that was filled with the small unassuming blossoms of pimpernel and eye-bright, he playfully drew a handful of Jessamine's brown curls through the green hedge and tied them with a knot of her own namesake-flowers.

'Now you can't get away!' he said merrily – 'I have fastened you up, and you are my little prisoner!'

She peered sideways over her shoulder at what he had done, and chuckled – then laughed till her pretty cheeks were dented all over with dancing dimples – and, perfectly satisfied with the arrangement, she settled herself down more comfortably among the leaves with a dove-like croon of pleasure.

'I told 'ee there wos a 'ole in the 'edge where I could creep froo!' – she said triumphantly – '*This* is the 'ole! It's allus bin 'ere. I've often coom'd when nobody's by, an' got roses for my own self. There be lots o' roses, bain't there?'

This with an inquiring glance, and suggestive pout.

Lionel took the hint, and springing up, ran to gather for her a posy of the prettiest half-open buds he could find – then, tying them up with a bit of string he had in his pocket, he knelt down again and gave them gently into her hands. She buried her tiny nose deep among the scented petals.

'O how bee-oo-ful!' she sighed – 'Ee'se a rare nice boy, Lylie! – I likes 'ee! Where's oor Drojunwors now?'

He laughed joyously –

'Just where they always were, dear, I expect!' he answered – 'I don't suppose anything will ever move them out of Homer's epic! It's always the same old story, you know!'

Jessamine nodded demurely.

'Always the same ole story!' she echoed with a comical plaintiveness – 'I 'member! – 'bout a bad lady, an' big men. Oh Lylie! There's a bee!'

She huddled herself and her roses up into a heap, her pretty little face expressive of the direst dismay as a big, boozy bumble-bee circled round and round her in apparent doubt as to whether she might not be some new specimen of floral growth, full of delicious honey – and Lionel, arming himself with a long fern-leaf, did manful battle with the winged epicurean till it became thoroughly convinced that these small pretty creatures were human beings, not flowers, and boomed lazily off on another quest for dainty novelties.

'Ee *wor* a bad bee!' said Jessamine, looking after the offending insect, and slowly relaxing her close-cuddled attitude – 'He's got all the flowers i' th' garden – an' they oughter be 'nuff for him wizout mine, oughtn't they?'

'Of course they ought!' agreed Lionel, feeling quite happy in the companionship of his little village friend, as he parted the dividing screen of flowers and leaves, and drew closer to her – 'Tell me Jessamine, did you come all by yourself across that big field over there?'

' 'Iss!' she replied proudly – 'The field's just 'tween th' church an' this big 'ouse where 'ee lives – Auntie Kate calls it "short cut". Sometimes it's full o' cows, an' I'se 'fraid of 'em – an' I can't coom – but today there's no cows, so I runned all th' way to see 'ee, Lylie!' and she looked at him affectionately – 'When's 'ee comin' to see me?'

Lionel's bright face clouded. 'I don't know, Jessamine!' he said sadly – 'I wish I could come – you don't think I wouldn't come if I could! – fast enough! But I have such a lot of lessons to do just now – they take up all my time – besides I'm not allowed to go anywhere except with the Professor.'

'The 'fessor? Wot's 'ee?' inquired Jessamine.

'He's my tutor – a very clever man who teaches me.'

Jessamine looked puzzled.

'Well, can't the 'fessor coom with 'ee? – an' see me an' my feyther?'

'I'm afraid he wouldn't care to – he's a very old man —'

'*I* know!' interrupted Jessamine with a nod of her head – 'He's a bad ole man – he doesn't want to see *me*! He's like the bad man i' th' fairy-book wot lost the babes i' th' wood – an' he's like 'oor feyther, Lylie! didn't 'ee say 'oor feyther would scold me if I came froo this 'edge, eh?'

'Yes – an I expect he would!' said Lionel.

'Then he's bad!' declared the small lady with emphasis. 'Nobody oughtn't to scold me, 'cos I'se allus tryin' to be good.' Then with a sudden change of tone, she added 'Poor Lylie! I'se so sorry for 'ee!'

There was something strangely moving in her voice, and Lionel, always sensitive, felt the tears rising very near his eyes.

'Why, dear?' he asked rather tremulously – while, to hide his feelings he busied himself in untying the twist he had made of her hair and the jessamine blossoms.

' 'Cos I fink you'se lonely – an' I'se 'fraid you won't see me never no more!'

And again she raised her blue eyes to the blue heavens, and looked as if she saw some dawning splendour there.

Lionel took both her little hands in his own and fondled them. There was a sadness at his heart, but not the kind of sadness she seemed to suggest.

'You mustn't say that, Jessamine,' – he murmured gently – 'I'll be sure to see you again often. Even when we go away from Combmartin, I shan't forget you. I shall come back and see you when I'm a big man.'

She peeped wistfully up at him.

'You'se be a long long time 'fore you'se a big man, Lylie!' she said.

He was silent. What she suggested was very true. It would indeed be a 'long long time' before the 'big man' stage of existence came to him, if it ever came to him at all. He was perfectly conscious within himself that he did not want to be a 'big man' – and that it was quite enough sadness for him to be a small boy. He could not realise the possibility of his living through years and years of work and worry, to attain this end of mere manhood – and then to go on through more years of worse work and worry, just to become old, wrinkled and toothless, and drop into the grave, forgetful of all that he had ever known, and senseless to the fact that he had ever existed. He was entirely aware that most people went through this kind of thing and didn't seem to mind it – but somehow it did not commend itself to him as his own particular destiny. If there were another life to be taken up after death, then he could understand the necessity there might be for living this one nobly – but the scientists had done away with that hope, and had declared death to be the only end of every soul's career. Thoughts such as these flitted vaguely through his brain while he knelt in front of Jessamine, holding her wee warm hands in his – she in turn regarding him seriously with her large, soft, angelic eyes.

Over the two children a silence and a shadow hung, inexplicable to themselves. Or was it not so much a shadow as a brightness? – made impressive by the very stillness of its approach and the mystic glory of its presence? It seemed incredible that the thorny and cruel ways of the world should be waiting to pierce and torture these innocent young lives – it was monstrous to imagine the dreamy-eyed, tender-hearted boy growing up into the usual type of modern man – the orthodox pattern demanded by the customs and conventionalities of his kind – and still more repellent was the idea that the sweet baby-girl with her pure look and heavenly smile, should be destined for the rough lot of a mere peasant drudge, so to pass her days and end them, without a touch of the finer essences which should nourish and expand all the delicate susceptibilities of her nature. Was there nothing better in store for these children than what we call life? Who could tell! If the deep charm which held them both mute, could have dissolved itself in music some answer might have been given; but God's meanings cannot be construed into the language of mortals; hence the reason of many expressive silences often encompassing us – silences more eloquent than speech. Presently Jessamine stirred uneasily in her nest of leaves.

'I'se goin' now, Lylie,' she announced.

'Oh, must you go so soon?' exclaimed Lionel – 'Can't you stay a little longer?'

Jessamine pursed up her rose lips with a gravely important air.

'I'se 'fraid not!' she said – 'I'se promised to fetch my feyther 'ome to dinner, an' 'ee'l be waitin' for me.'

'Well, will you come back again, this afternoon?' urged the boy – 'Come back about four o'clock, and I'll be here to see you.'

The little maid looked coquettishly doubtful.

'I doesn't know 'bout that!' she murmured, coyly – 'My ole 'oss 'spects me this arternoon.'

'But you *might* leave the old horse for once to come to me!' pleaded Lionel – 'You know I may have to go away altogether from Combmartin soon!'

' 'Iss!' sighed Jessamine, her eyes drooping demurely –
then with a quick brightening of her face she added – 'Well,
I'll try, Lylie. P'r'aps I'll come an' p'r'aps I won't be able to
come. But I'm sure I'll see 'ee soon again; I won't 'ave to
wait till you'se a big man. I'll see 'ee long 'fore then. 'Ee
mustn't forgit me, Lylie!'

'Forget you! Certainly not!' responded the boy almost
ardently, as he set the little white-sunbonnet straight on her
head, and tied the strings of it under her pretty chin – 'I
shall never, never forget you, dear little Jessamine!'

She pushed herself further through the hedge on her hands
and knees, and smiled up at him.

'Wouldn't 'ee like to kiss me 'gain, Lylie?' she demanded,
with ineffable sweetness.

For answer he put his arms round her neck, all among the
blossoms, and tenderly pressed the little cherry of a mouth
so frankly uplifted to his own.

'Good-bye, Lylie!' she said then, beginning to scramble out
from among the leaves.

'Good-bye, Jessamine! But not for long!' he answered.

'Not for long!' she echoed – 'You'se *sure* not to forget me,
Lylie!'

'Sure!' declared the boy, smiling at her somewhat sadly,
as she now stood upright behind the hedge, and her little
figure could only dimly be seen through the close network of
leaves. She turned to go – then on a sudden impulse ran back,
and with her two hands made a round peep-hole through the
trailing sprays of jessamine, so that her winsome baby face
looked literally framed in her own blossoms.

'Good-bye, Lylie! Not for long!' she said.

And with that she disappeared.

Left alone once more, Lionel did not feel quite so happy
as he had done before his little visitor came. Somehow the
pretty child's quick departure grieved him – he longed to
break through the boundary hedge and run after her, and

have another long and happy day of rest and freedom – but he had given his 'word of honour' to his father not to leave the grounds, and he manfully resisted the sore temptation that beset him. Yet certain it was that with Jessamine the light of the landscape seemed to have fled; – a sense of desolation oppressed him; and to distract his thoughts he took up the two books he had left on the garden-seat, and set himself to study them. But in vain – his mind wandered – he could not fix his attention – and he began watching the graceful movements of two butterflies that flew in and out among the roses – pale-blue pretty creatures, like cornflowers on wings. And all at once the terrible callousness of nature forced itself upon his attention as it had never done before, and filled him with gloom.

'Nothing cares!' he thought – 'If the best and wisest person that ever lived were in trouble, or were to die, everything would go on just the same; – the birds would sing and the butterflies dance, and the flowers grow, and the sun shine. I suppose that is really why they have fixed upon an Atom as the first cause of it all – you can't expect an Atom to care!'

He moved slowly down the path, and went towards the carriage-drive, where plenty of deep shade was cast by a double row of broad and full-foliaged elms. Outside the closed carriage-gate he saw, through the bars, a man standing, holding a basket in one hand, and making uncouth signs to him with the other. He advanced quickly – then as quickly stopped, as he more plainly perceived the hideous aspect of the unhappy creature who confronted him – a miserable human deformity, with twisted tottering limbs, protruding lack-lustre eyes and a deathly grin upon the wide mouth, which through illness, idiocy, or both, slobbered and mumbled continuously and incoherently. The head of the wretched man jerked to and fro with an incessant convulsive motion – in the basket he carried were a number of exquisite white roses, together with several large, beautifully polished rosy apples, the fresh loveliness of these natural products forming a strange and cruel contrast to the appearance of their ragged and miserable vendor, who continued to beckon Lionel with his twitching hand, smiling that fixed and ghastly smile of his which, no doubt, he meant, poor fellow, as an expression of deference and goodwill. But the boy, chilled to the marrow by the sight of such an unexpected image of horror in human shape, stood stock still for a minute, staring – then turning, he ran with all his might into the house, and up to the school-room, every pulse in his body throbbing with nervous shock and repulsion.

'Oh, it is quite right – it must be right!' he gasped, as he flung himself down in a chair and tried to forget the gruesome figure he had just seen – 'It *is* an Atom that created everything! – it couldn't be a Person! No Person with pity or kindness, could allow such a poor dreadful man as that to live on, and suffer! A good God would have killed him!'

He shuddered, hiding his face in his hands. His forehead throbbed and burned – the burden of the horror of merely human things suddenly came down upon him, and seemed greater than he could bear. Human toil, human torture, human weakness, human helplessness, all endured for nothing! – and only to end in death! Life then was a mere rack, in which poor humanity was bound, tormented and slain – uselessly! – for so indeed must Life appear to all who leave God out of it, or set Him aside as an unknown quantity. He got up, and walked to and fro restlessly.

'How wicked it is!' he mused, his young soul fired with strange and feverish indignation – 'How vile! – to make us live against our wills! We didn't ask to come into the world – it is shameful we should be sent here. Unless there were some reason for it – but there's none; if there were one, it would surely be explained. A reasonable Person would explain it. Reuben Dale believes there's a reason and think's it's all right – but then he's quite ignorant – he doesn't know any better. I wonder what he would say about that beggar-man? – could he tell why his God made such a dreadful creature?'

He stopped in his uneasy rambling, and struck by a sudden thought, went downstairs in search of a particular book. He looked in the drawing-room, and in his father's study, and everywhere where books were kept, but vainly – then, still possessed by the one idea he went along the stone passage that led to the back of the house and the servants' offices, and called one of the housemaids who had always been rather kind to him.

'Lucy! Are you there?'

'Yes, Master Lionel! What is it?'

'Have you got a Testament you can lend me? I want to look at it for just a few minutes.'

'Why, certainly!' And Lucy, a bright wholesome-faced girl of about twenty came out of the kitchen, smiling – 'I'll lend you my school-prize one, Master Lionel – I know you'll take great care of it.'

'That I will!' the boy assured her, whereupon she tripped away, and soon retured with a book carefully wrapped up in white tissue-paper. She unfolded this, and showed a handsome morocco-bound square volume, bearing its title in letters of gold – 'New Testament.'

'Don't you ink it, there's a dear!' she said – 'And give it to me back when you've done with it.'

Lionel nodded, and returning to the school-room, shut the door. Then, with a fluttering heart, he opened the book. What he was looking for he soon found – the story of Christ healing the lepers. Leprosy, he had been taught, was the most frightful disease known – both hereditary and infectious, it was a deadly scourge that tortured the limbs, distorted the countenance and made of the human frame a thing *in*human and ghastly – yet Christ never turned away in loathing from any miserable creature so afflicted. On the contrary He healed

all who came to Him, and sent them on their way rejoicing –
yet on one such occasion, when ten lepers were cleansed, only
one returned to give thanks to his great Benefactor. Lionel
felt that there was something more in this narrative than was
quite apparent in the mere reading of it – something subtle
and significant, which he could not quite grasp, though he
began to reason with himself – 'Is it because we are ungrateful
that life is made cruel for us – or what is it?'

His head ached and his eyes smarted – he closed the Testament sorrowfully, and with a deep sigh. 'It's no use to me' –
he said – 'Because though it's all very beautiful, my father
says it isn't true. And in one of the books I have, the writer
who is a very clever man, says it isn't at all certain that Christ
ever existed, and that it was Peter and Paul who invented
Him. Oh dear me! I wish I knew *what* to believe – because
even in the scientific arguments no one man agrees with the
other. It's all a muddle, whichever way you turn!'

He went downstairs again, and returned the Testament to
its owner with a gentle,

'Thank you, Lucy.'

'Did you find what you wanted, Master Lionel?' asked the
good-natured girl.

'Not exactly!' he answered – 'But it's all right, Lucy' –
here he hesitated – 'Lucy, did you see a beggar-man selling
roses and apples just now outside the carriage-gate? – he was
all twisted on one side, and had such a dreadful face!'

'Poor fellow!' said Lucy pityingly – 'Yes, Master Lionel –
I often see him. He's the "silly man" of the village – the
children call him "Hoddy-Doddy". But he's not a beggar,
though he's more than half-witted – he's a rare good heart of
his own, and an idea of what's right and honest, for he manages
to make his own living and is a burden to nobody. It's wonderful how he manages it – I suppose God looks after him, for
no one else does.'

'God looks after him!' This gave Lionel new subject-matter for reflection, and he returned to the school-room, slowly and thoughtfully. His dinner was brought up to him there, and afterwards he set himself to work at his lessons assiduously. Hot head and trembling hands did not deter him from application – and he worked on so steadily that he never knew how time went, till a sudden sick giddiness seized him, and he was obliged to get up and go out in the garden for fresh air lest he should faint. He found then that it was four o'clock, and remembering that he had asked Jessamine to come back to the ' 'ole in th' 'edge' at that hour, he went to the appointed spot, and waited there patiently till nearly five. But the little maiden did not appear, – and he was quite down-hearted and weary with disappointment, as well as with overwork, when at last he went in to his tea. Lucy had prepared that meal for him, and she stood looking at him somewhat compassionately as he listlessly threw off his cap and approached the table.

'I should get to bed early if I were you, Master Lionel;' – she said kindly – 'You look quite tired and wore out, that you do.'

'I want to wait up till mother comes home,' he answered.

Lucy fidgeted about, and seemed uneasy in her mind at this.

'Oh, I think you'd better not,' she observed; 'Your pa'd be very angry if you did. You know you're always to be in bed by nine, and your ma said she couldn't possibly get back before eleven. You go to bed like a good boy, or you'll get us all into trouble.'

'Very well!' he said, with an indifferent air – 'I don't mind! After all, it isn't as if she cared, you know. If she *cared* – ' here quite suddenly his lip began to tremble, and to his own amazement and indignation, he burst out crying.

The warm-hearted Lucy had her arms round him in a minute.

'Why, what's the matter, dear?' she asked caressingly,

drawing the sobbing boy to her good womanly breast – 'Lor' sakes! – how you're trembling! There, there! don't cry, don't cry ! you're tired; – that's what it is. Poor little fellow! – you've got too many lessons to learn, and too little play. I'm real sorry, that I am, that Mr. Montrose has gone away.'

'So am I;' murmured Lionel very much ashamed of his own emotion, though he was child enough to feel a certain pleasure and comfort in having Lucy's kind arm round him – 'I liked Mr. Montrose.' Here he choked back his tears, and fingered Lucy's brooch, which was a brilliant masterpiece of the village silversmith's skill, being a heart with a long dagger run through it, the said dagger having the name 'Lucy' engraved on its harmless point. 'Who gave you that, Lucy?'

'My young man,' – replied Lucy with a giggle; 'I'm the dagger, and I'm supposed to have run right through his heart – don't you see? Isn't it funny?'

'Very funny!' agreed Lionel, beginning to smile faintly.

Lucy giggled afresh.

'That's what I said when he gave it to me – but he was very cross and told me it wasn't funny at all – it was poetry. You're feeling better now, aren't you dear?'

'Oh yes!' and Lionel dried his eyes on her apron – 'Don't mind me, Lucy. I'm only a little tired, as you say. I'll have my tea now.'

He sat down to the table and made such a brave show of being hungry, that Lucy soon withdrew, quite satisfied. But when she had gone he ceased eating, and went to his old seat in the window, there to dream and muse. He tried conscientiously, before the evening closed in, to study some more of the 'subjects' Professor Cadman-Gore had left for his consideration, but he could not – his head swam directly he bent over a printed page, so he gave up the attempt in despair. He watched the sun sink, and the stars come out, and then went willingly enough to bed. Before he shut his little bedroom-window he heard an owl hoot among the nieghbouring woods, and thought what a pitiful cry it uttered.

'Perhaps it is like me, wondering why it was ever made!' he said to himself – 'And perhaps it thinks the Atom as cruel as I do!'

CHAPTER 9

TIRED out as he was, sleep came reluctantly to Lionel's eyes that night. There was an odd quick palpitation behind his brows, which teased him for a long time and would not let him rest – it seemed to him like a little mill for ever turning and grinding out portions of facts which he had recently committed to memory – bits of history, bits of grammar, bits of Euclid, bits of Latin, bits of Greek – till he began to wonder how all the bits would piece themselves together and make a comprehensive ground-work for further instruction. By-and-by he found himself considering how very stupid it was of Richard Coeur de Lion to make so much fuss over the Holy Sepulchre, when now there were so many clever men alive who were all agreed that Christ was a myth, and that there never was any Holy Sepulchre at all! What a very dense king was Richard! – what a brave dunce! – with his perpetual oath 'Par le Splendeur de Dieu!' While all the time, if he had only known it, the Atom was just a thing with no 'Splendeur de Dieu' about it! And oh, what a wicked waste of life there had been – what terrific martyrdoms for the 'Faith' – merely to end in an age which was scientifically prepared to deny and utterly condemn all spiritual and supernatural beliefs whatsoever! Gradually and by gentle degrees, Coeur de Lion and the 'Splendeur de Dieu,' and the Atom, and Jessamine Dale, with bits of facts, and bits of Professor Cadman-Gore's unhandsome features curiously joined on to the dreadful physiognomy of the 'silly man' of the village, got jumbled all together in inextricable confusion, and the little tiresome mill in his head turned slower and slower, and presently ceased to grind – and he fell into a profound slumber – the deep, stirless trance of utter exhaustion. So dead asleep was he that a voice calling 'Lylie! Lylie!' only reached his consciousness at last as though it were a faint far-off sound in a dream – and not till the call had been repeated many times did he start up, rubbing his heavy eyelids, and gazing in speechless alarm at a mysterious cloaked figure bending over his bed. The room was dark save for the moonlight that struck one wide slanting beam across the floor, and he could not for a moment imagine what strange and spectral visitant thus roused him from his rest. But before he had time to think, the figure's arms were round him, and its voice murmured tenderly,

'Lylie? Have I frightened you? – Poor boy! – poor baby! Don't you know me?'

'Mother!' And in his sudden surprise and joy he sprang up half out of bed to return her embrace. 'How good of you to come and see me! – and you haven't even taken your hat and cloak off! Did Lucy tell you I wanted to wait up for you?'

'No – Lucy didn't tell me' – answered Mrs. Valliscourt, drawing him more closely to her breast; 'Poor child, how thin you are! Such a little bag o' bones! You mustn't catch cold – curl yourself under my cloak, so! There! Now Lylie, I want you to be very quiet, and listen to me attentively, will you?'

'Yes, mother!'

Cuddled under the warm cloak, with her arms round him, Lionel was in a state of perfect happiness – this unexpected nocturnal visit seemed too good to be true. He was secretly astonished, but entirely glad – he had never dreamed of the possibility of so much consolation and delight.

'You feel so small!' said his mother then, with a tremulous laugh – 'In your little nightgown you seem just a mere bundle of a baby – the very same sort of bundle I used to carry about and be so proud of. You *were* a baby once, you know!'

Lionel nestled closer and kissed her soft hand.

'Yes, mother, I suppose I was!'

'Well, now Lylie,' she went on, speaking rapidly and in low

130

tones – 'You must try to understand all I say to you. I am going away, dear – for a time . . . on a visit . . . with a friend who wishes to make me happy. I'm not very happy just at present . . . neither are you I daresay . . . you see your father is exceptionally clever and good' – and her voice here rang with a delicate inflection of mockery – 'and – very naturally – he does not care much for people who are not equally clever and good – so it makes it difficult to get on with him sometimes. He does not like me to sing and dance and amuse myself any more than he likes you to play games with other boys. You are too young to go about by yourself and have a good time yet – but by-and-by you will grow up, and you will know what a good time means. You will find out that when people get very, very dull, and are almost ready to kill themselves for dullness, their doctors advise them to have a change of scenery, and a change of society. That's what I want. Good people like your father, never want a change – I'm not good, and I do!'

Lionel began to feel pained and perplexed.

'You *are* good, mother!' he said, with emphasis.

'No, darling, I'm not' – she answered quickly – 'And that is just what I want to impress upon you. I'm not good; – I'm a bad, selfish, cold-hearted woman. I don't love anybody – not even you!'

'Oh, mother!' The little cry was piteous, like that of a wounded bird.

She stooped and gathered him up suddenly in her arms, lifting him completely out of bed – and holding him thus with an almost passionate tenderness, rocked him to and fro as if he were the merest infant.

'No!' she said, a mingled scorn and sweetness thrilling in her voice – 'No – I don't love my baby at all – I never did! I never had any heart, Lylie – never! I never rocked you in my arms like this all day, and kissed your dear little rosy feet and hands, and sang you to sleep with all the funny little nonsense songs I know! No, my pet! I never loved you – I never did – I never shall!'

And bending down, she kissed him again and again with a burning force and fervour that frightened him. He dared not move, she clasped him so convulsively – and he dared not speak, for as the moonbeams glittered on her face he saw that she was deadly pale, and that her eyes looked wild; – he feared she was ill – an instinctive feeling that something terrible was about to happen made his heart beat fast, and he trembled violently.

'Are you cold, dear?' she murmured, sitting down in a chair by the bed, and still holding him jealously in her embrace – 'There!' and she drew the ample folds of her fur-lined cloak more snugly around him with all the cosseting fondness of an adoring mother – 'That's cosier, isn't it, little one? Now, let me finish my talk. You know, Lylie dear, when you were a baby, I used to have you all to myself, and that made a great difference to me – I was quite happy then. I used to plan such pretty things for you – I had so many hopes too – oh, so many! I was only a girl when you came to me, and girls often have pretty fancies. And you were such a darling baby – so plump, and round, and rosy – and merry! – oh, so merry! And I was very proud of you, and very jealous too – I used to nurse you and dress you all myself, because I could not bear the idea of any common paid woman taking care of you. And when you began to speak, I did not want you to be taught lessons – I wanted you to play all day and grow big and strong – just as I often wanted to dance and sing myself. But your father made up his mind that you were to be a very clever man, and he had you taught all sorts of things as soon as you could spell. And so gradually I lost my baby. And I never cared – afterwards. I cared a good deal at first, because I saw you were getting thin and pale and tired-looking; – but it was no use – so I gave up caring. I don't care now – because you see you are growing quite a man, Lylie, though you are not eleven yet – poor little man! – and you won't want me at all. I am only in your way, and I am always vexing your father and making trouble by giving my opinions about you and your studies. That is one of the reasons why I am going on this – this visit – just to enjoy myself a little. If it hadn't been for you, I shouldn't have come back here to-night – but I couldn't go without bidding my boy good-bye – I couldn't!'

She said this wildly – great tears filled her eyes and dropped heavily one by one among Lionel's curls. He sat up in her arms, his little bare feet dangling down from her knee, and put one hand coaxingly against her cheek.

'Are you really going tonight, mother? So late?' he asked plaintively – 'Must you go?'

She looked straight at him, and smiled through her tears.

'Yes, I must! I want a good time for once in my life, Lylie – and I'm going to have it! I'm like you – I want a long holiday – no lessons, and no tutors!'

A sense of impending desolation filled his soul.

'Oh mother, I wish you'd take me with you!' he said – 'I do love you so much!'

What strange expression was that which darkened her beautiful face? Was it guilt, shame or despair? – or all three in one foreboding shadow?

'You love me so much? Poor boy, do you? It is strange – for I've given you little cause to love me! You mustn't do it, Lylie! – it's a mistake! – and – tomorrow your father will tell you why.'

She was silent a minute – then, glancing at the little feet that gleamed in the moonbeams, frail and white against her dark draperies, she took them both in her hands and kissed them.

'Poor, cold little tootsies!' she said, laughing nervously, though the tears still glistened on her cheeks – 'I mustn't keep you too long out of bed. See here, Lylie,' – and she drew a small soft parcel from her pocket – 'I want you to keep this in some safe place for me – till – till I come back; – it is the only remembrance I have of my baby – when you *were* a baby. I was a very proud little mamma, as I have told you – and no sash in any of the London shops seemed good enough or pretty enough for my boy. So I had this one specially woven on one of the French looms after my own design, for you to wear with your little white frocks. It is blue silk, and the pattern on it is a daisy chain. Don't let your father see it, but keep it for me till I return and ask you for it. I don't feel like taking it with me – where I am going. See – I'll put it under your pillow, and you must hide it somewhere in the morning – will you?'

'Yes, mother. But – but will you be long away?'

He asked this timidly, bewildered and frightened by he knew not what.

'I don't know, darling,' – she answered evasively. 'It all depends! Your father will give you all the news of me! And he will be sure to tell you that you mustn't love me, Lylie! – do you hear that? You mustn't love me!'

'But I shall,' – he said gently – 'Nobody can prevent it. I shall always love you.'

She sat very still a moment – the brooding shadow heavy on her face.

'You think so now,' – she murmured, more to herself than to him – 'Poor boy – you think so now – but when you know – '

Then she caught him close to her breast, and kissed him.

'Now for the downy nest!' she said, lifting him up, and laying him tenderly back into bed again, her eyes resting upon him with a miserable yearning, though she forced a strange distraught smile – 'All the moonlight shines on your pale face, Lylie, and you look – oh, you look like a little dead child, my darling – like a little dead child!'

And suddenly falling to her knees, she threw her arms

across the bed and dropping her head upon them, sobbed as though her heart were breaking.

Poor Lionel shivered in every limb with alarm and distress – his sensitive soul was racked by his mother's anguish, though it was incomprehensible to him – and he felt as if indeed it would be better to die than to see her thus.

'Don't cry, mother!' he faltered at last, faintly; 'Oh don't cry!'

She raised herself, and dried her eyes with a handkerchief from which the delicate odour of violets came floating, sweet as the breath of the living flowers.

'No – I won't cry, darling!' she answered, beginning to laugh hysterically, 'I don't know really why I should, because I am quite happy – quite!' And rising to her feet, she fastened her cloak about her with hands that trembled greatly – Lionel saw the diamonds on her white fingers shake like drops of dew about to fall – 'I'm going to have a splendid time and enjoy myself thoroughly!' – this she said with a curiously defiant air – 'and whatever happens afterwards may happen as it likes – I don't care!' She repeated the words with hard emphasis. '*I don't care!* Years ago I should have cared – dreadfully – but I've been taught not to care, and now I don't. "Don't Care" was hung, they say – but as far as I'm concerned, it really doesn't matter whether one's hung, or drowned, or dies of a fever or a surfeit – it's all the same a hundred years hence!' She lifted her hands to her head, and with a coquettish touch settled the small velvet hat she wore, more becomingly on her clustering hair – while Lionel looking up at her from his pillow, saw all her wonderful beauty transfigured, as it were, in the ethereal radiance of the moon, and as he looked he felt, by some strange instinct, that he must try to hold her back from some unknown yet menacing peril.

'Mother, don't go!' he pleaded – 'Stay tonight, at any rate! Wait till tomorrow – oh, do, mother! Don't leave me!'

He stretched out his emaciated little arms – and his eyes,

full of child-yearning and student thought commingled, appealed to her with a speechless eloquence. She bent over him again, and taking his hands, pressed them close to her bosom.

'Dear, if I had any heart I shouldn't leave you' – she said – 'I know that! But I have none – not a scrap. I want you to remember this, and then you will not feel at all sad about me. People without hearts always get on best in this world. Your mother used to have a heart – full of romance, and nonsense, and sentiment, and faith, Lylie! – yes, dear, even faith. Your mother was a very ignorant woman once, so ignorant as to actually believe in a God! You know how angry your father is with silly folks who believe in a God? Well, he soon got me out of all those foolish ways, and taught me that the only necessary rule of life was Respectability. Oh, you don't know how dull Respectability can be! – how insufferably hopelessly *dull*! You don't know – you can't understand, that when the only object in life is to be respectable and nothing more – no other ambition, no other future, no other end – it becomes deadly! – even desperate! You can't understand – you are too young – poor Lylie! – you are only a child – and I'm talking to you as if you are a man. Good-bye, dear! Love me for tonight – you *may* love me a little, just till morning comes – I like to think you are loving me! – Good-bye!'

He clung round her neck.

'Don't go, mother!' he whispered.

She kissed him passionately.

'I must, Lylie! I should die or go mad if I didn't. I am tired to death – I want a change!'

'But you won't be long away?' he murmured, still holding her fast.

'Not long,' – she replied mechanically; 'Not long! See, I'll make you a promise, Lylie! – I'll come back directly your father sends for me!' – and she laughed – a little cold, mirthless laugh which somehow chilled Lionel's blood – 'My little boy –

my pet – you must not cling to me so! – you hurt me! – I cannot bear it – oh, I cannot bear it!'

A faint cry that was half a sob, escaped her, and she almost roughly unloosened his arms from about her neck, and put him back on his pillow. He was pained and bewildered.

'Did I really hurt you, mother?' he asked, wistfully.

'Yes – you really hurt me! You – you pulled my hair'; – and she smiled, her beautiful eyes shining down upon him like stars in the semi-darkness – 'And I felt as though your little fingers were pulling at my heart too! Only I have no heart! – I forgot that – but *you* mustn't forget it!' She paused – for at that moment the crunching noise of wheels was heard outside on the gravel of the carriage-drive – and she listened, with a strange wild look of expectation on her face.

'You've read all about the French Revolution, Lylie, haven't you? Oh yes, poor little mannikin, I know you have! – I daresay you've got all the troubles of Louis Seize by heart. You remember when the tumbrils or death-carts used to come rattling along the streets, to fetch the people for execution? Well, I heard the wheels of *my* death-cart just now – it has come for *me* – and *I'm* going to execution, by choice, not by compulsion!'

Roused to sudden energy, Lionel sprang up in his bed.

Mother, mother, you shan't go!' he exclaimed, quite desperately – 'I'll come with you if you do! – you mustn't leave me behind!'

Her fair features hardened, as with a determined grasp she caught hold of him and laid him down again.

'Naughty boy!' she said sharply – 'You'll make me very angry, and I shall be sorry I came to see you and say goodnight. Lie still, and go to sleep. If you love me, you must obey me!'

Shivering a little, he turned from her, and hid his face in the pillow, shrinking from the imperious regard of those wonderful eyes of hers, which could flash with wrath as well as deepen with tenderness – and the old dull sense that he was nothing to her, and less than nothing, stole upon him almost unawares. Presently, moved by quick penitence, she stooped towards him, and ran her fingers caressingly through his curls.

'There! I did not mean to be cross, Lylie! Forgive me! And kiss me good-bye, darling!'

Silently he put his arms round her – the moonlight fell pallidly across the bed, spectrally illuminating the faces of both child and mother – on the one was written with touching pathos, the last hopeless, helpless appeal of innocence and grief – on the other a reckless resolve, and a callous, despairing self-contempt. Life gone to waste and ruin through lovelessness and neglect; – such was the history declared in every line of Helen Valliscourt's countenance, as she clasped her boy once more to her breast, kissing him on lips, cheeks and brow, and ruffling the thick soft clusters of his hair with loving lingering fingers.

'Good-bye! – good-bye!' she whispered – 'I have no heart – or it would break, Lylie! Good-bye, my pet – my baby! Love me till tomorrow – good-bye!'

With this last 'good-bye' – she tore herself resolutely away from him – and before he could quite realise it, she had gone. He lay still for a moment trembling – then on a sudden impulse left his bed, and ran bare-footed out on the landing, where he paused at the top of the stairs, frightened and irresolute. All was dark and silent.

'Mother!' he called faintly. A door swung to with a creaking groan and rattle – a rising wind sighed through the crevices.

'Mother!'

The plaintive cry was swallowed up and lost in the darkness – but as he listened, with every nerve strained and every sense on the alert, he heard the noise of trotting horses' hoofs and carriage wheels, apparently retreating at a rapid rate up the Combmartin road. He rushed back to his room, and hastily opening the window, looked out. It was full moonlight – every object in the landscape was as clearly defined as in broad day – but not a trace of any human creature was visible. The night air was chilly, and his teeth chattered with cold – but he was hardly aware of this, so great was the burden of sorrow and desolation that had fallen on his heart. He raised his eyes to the clear sky – one splendid star, whose glowing lustre was scarcely lessened by the rays of the moon, shone immediately opposite to him like a silver sanctuary-lamp in Heaven. Owls hooted, answering each other with dismal persistence, and scared bats fluttered in and out among the trees, which were now beginning to sway languidly to and fro in a light breeze coming up from the sea. And the impression of disaster and gloom deepened in the boy's soul – and once again from his trembling lips came the piteous wailing cry.

'Mother! Oh, mother!'

Then a great rush of tears blinded his sight – and feeling his way back to bed through the salt haze of that bitter falling rain, he shiveringly huddled himself into a forlorn little heap of misery, and sobbed himself to sleep.

CHAPTER 10

NEXT morning he showed few signs of the grief he had suffered during the night. True, he was much paler than usual, and very silent – but being well accustomed to hide his emotions and keep his troubles to himself, he complained of nothing, not even to Lucy when, as she brought him his breakfast she said, in rather a flurried manner:

'Your ma came home last night, Master Lionel, and went away again – what do you think of that?'

'I don't think anything' – he replied wearily; 'Why should I? It's not my business.'

Lucy hesitated. Should she tell him what all the servants in the house too truly suspected! – what the very villagers in Combmartin were already gossiping about at their cottage doors and in the common room of the inn?

'No, I can't do it!' she mentally decided – 'He looks as white as a little ghost, he do, and I won't bother him. He wouldn't understand maybe, and he's got all his lessons to learn, poor little chap, and it'll only unsettle him. Anyhow he'll hear it fast enough!' Aloud she said, 'I suppose your pa and the Professor will be home by the first coach from Lynton this morning?'

'I suppose so,' assented Lionel indifferently.

'I don't like Lynton myself,' went on Lucy – 'People talk about it a lot, but it's just a nasty, damp, up-and-down place without any real comfort in it. They've got a queer tram-car now that slides up the hill from Lynmouth to Lynton, and *that* doesn't make it any prettier I can tell you!' She paused; then added by way of a totally irrelevant after-thought, 'There's a letter addressed to your pa in your ma's writing, waiting for him on his study-table.'

Lionel remained silent, pretending to be entirely absorbed

in the enjoyment of his breakfast. Lucy, finding he was not inclined to talk, soon left him to himself, much to his relief, for when quite alone he was free to push away the food that nauseated him to even look at, and to think his own thoughts without interruption. His mother's strange visit to his bedside during the night – her stranger words, her tears, her kisses, seemed this morning more like the vague impressions of a dream than a reality – and unless he had found the sash – his own baby-sash – she had left with him, under his pillow, he would have been inclined to doubt the whole incident. As it was, he was afraid to dwell too much upon it, for he had a horrible presentiment that it meant something more than he dared formulate – something dreadful – something hopeless – something that for him, would bring great misery. He had carefully hidden away the 'baby-sash' – a four-yards' length of broad soft ribbon, with the delicate design of a daisy-chain straying over its pale blue silken ground – he had looked at it first with critical interest, wondering what he had been like when as an infant he had worn such a pretty thing, and noting that it was scented with the same delicious odour of violets that had been wafted from his mother's handkerchief, when she had dried her eyes after her sudden fit of weeping. Having put it by in a safe place he knew of, he went to his books and set himself desperately to work, in order to try to forget his own disquietude. Beginning by translating a passage of Virgil into English blank verse, he went on to 'Caesar's Comment-aries,' – then he did several difficult and puzzling sums, and was stretching every small fibre of his young brain well on the rack of learning, when a coach-horn sounded, and he saw the Lynton coach itself come rattling down-hill into Combmartin. His father and Professor Cadman-Gore were on top – that he saw at a glance – and in another few minutes he, taking cautious peeps from the school-room window, perceived their two familiar figures walking up the drive and entering the house. And now – something seemed to stop the boy from the resumption of his tasks – a curious sensation came over him as though he were imperiously bidden to wait and hear the worst. What worst? He could not analyse any 'worst' satisfactorily to himself – yet. . . .

A violent ringing of bells in the outside corridor startled him and set his heart beating rapidly – he got up from his chair and stood, anxiously listening and wondering what was the matter. All at once his father's voice pitched in a high hoarse key of utmost wrath, called loudly:

'Lionel! Lionel! Where is the boy? Has he turned tramp, as his mother has turned — '

The sentence was left unfinished, for at that moment, Lionel ran down the stairs quickly and faced him.

'I am here, father!'

He trembled as he spoke, for he thought his father had suddenly gone mad. Crimson with fury, his eyes rolling wildly in his head, his wolfish teeth clenched on his under-lip, he was a terrible sight to see – and his fiendish aspect overwhelmed poor Lionel with such alarm that he scarcely perceived the Professor, who stood in the background, cracking his great knuckles together and widening his mouth into a strangely sardonic grin. Directly his little son appeared, Mr. Valliscourt pulled himself up as it were by a violent effort, and bringing his eyebrows together so that they met in a hard black line on the bridge of his nose, he said in choked fierce accents:

'Oh, you *are* here! Did you — ' he paused, took breath, and resumed – 'Did you see your mother yesterday?'

'Yes' – answered the boy faintly – 'I saw her last night. I was in bed and she came and woke me up, and said good-bye to me.'

Mr. Valliscourt glared at the fragile trembling little figure in frowning scorn.

'Said good-bye to you! Was that all? – or was there anything else? Speak out!'

Lionel's teeth began to chatter with fear.

'She said – she said she was going on a visit with – with a friend who would make her happy' – here a deep and awful oath sprang from Mr. Valliscourt's lips, causing the Professor to cough loudly by way of remonstrance – 'and – and – she said she was not very happy just now, and that she wanted a change. She said she would not be gone long, and she cried very much, and kissed me. And she promised she would come back as soon as you sent for her. Oh dear! – whatever *is* the matter? Oh, father, do tell me, please!'

He staggered a little – his head swam – and he lost breath.

'Yes, I *will* tell you!' cried his father furiously – 'I will tell you truths, as she has told you lies! Your mother is a vile woman! – a wretch – a drab! – a disgrace to me and to you! Do you know what it is when a wife leaves her husband and runs away like a thief in the night with another man? If you do *not* know, you must learn – for this is what your mother has done! The "friend" who is to "make her happy",' and Mr. Valliscourt's angry visage darkened with a hideous sneer – 'is Sir Charles Lascelles, the fashionable pet black-guard of society – she has gone with him – she will never come back! She has dishonoured my name, and glories in her dis-honour! Never think of her again – never speak of her! From this day, remember you have *no* mother!'

Lionel put up his trembling little hands to his head as though he sought to shield himself from a storm of blows. His heart beat wildly – he tired to speak but could not. He stared helplessly at Professor Cadman-Gore, and half fancied he saw a gleam of something like pity flicker across the wrinkled and sour physiognomy of that learned man – but all was blurred and dim before his sight – and the only distinct things he realised were the horror of his father's face and the still greater horror of his father's words.

'You know the meaning of a shamed life?' – went on Mr. Valliscourt ruthlessly – 'Young as you are, you have read in history how there have been men – and women too – who have chosen to die, rather than live disgraced. Not so your mother! She delights in her wickedness – she elects to live in open immorality rather than in honour. In her wanton selfishness she has thought nothing either of me or of you. She is thoroughly bad – in olden times she would have been set in the pillory, or whipped at the cart's tail! And richly would she have deserved such punishment!' and as he spoke his right hand clenched suddenly, as though in imagination he held the scourge he would fain have used to bruise and scarify the flesh of his erring wife – 'When you are a man, you will blush to think she ever was your mother! She has made herself a scandal to society – she is a debased and degraded example of impudence, dishonesty and infamy! – she — '

But here Lionel stumbled forward giddily, and laid his weak little hand appealingly on his father's arm.

'Oh no, father, no! I can't bear it – I can't bear it!' he cried – 'I love her! – I love her! – I do indeed! – I can't help it. She kissed me – only last night, father! – yes, and she took me in her arms – oh, I can't forget it – I can't, really! – I love her – I do! – Oh mother – mother!'

Stammering thus incoherently, he saw his father's eyes flame upon him like balls of fire – his father's form seemed to dilate all at once to twice its natural dimensions – indistinctly he heard the growing voice of the Professor interpose with the words – 'The boy has had enough – let him be! ... then, on a blind impulse he ran, ran, ran headlong out of the house – not knowing in the least where he was going, but only bent on getting away – somewhere – anywhere – only away! Down Combmartin road he rushed panting, like a little escaped mad thing, the noonday sun beating hot on his uncovered head – as in a wild vision he heard voices calling him and saw strange faces looking at him – till suddenly he became aware of a familiar figure approaching him – a figure he dimly recognised as that of his old acquaintance, Clarinda Cleverly

Payne, who he had never seen since his tutor Montrose had left Combmartin. Running straight towards her, he cried aloud:

'Oh Miss Payne! – it isn't true, is it? Oh do tell me! – it can't be true! My mother hasn't gone away for ever, has she? – oh no, surely not! Oh no, no, no! She loves me – I know she does! She would not leave me – she wouldn't I'm sure! Oh do tell me, dear Miss Payne! – *you* do not think she is wicked, do you?'

Over the weather-beaten face of the kindly Clarinda came an expression of the deepest, aye, almost divine compassion. In one moment, her womanly soul comprehended the child's torture – his bewilderment, his grief, his exceeding loneliness – and without a word in answer, she opened her arms. But Lionel, gazing at her in passionate suspense, met the solemn and pitying look of her eyes – a look that confirmed all his worst fears – and sick to the very heart, seeing the sky, the earth, and the distant sea all gather together in one great avalanche of blackness that came rolling down upon him, he staggered another step forward, and fell senseless at her feet.

'BETTER take him away for a few days,' said Dr. Hartley, a brisk bright-looking type of the country physician, as he held his watch in one hand, and felt Lionel's feeble pulse with the other. 'Give him a little change – move him about a bit. He's had a sort of nervous shock – yes – yes – very sad! – I heard the news in the village . . . shocking – unhappily these domestic troubles are becoming very common . . . most distressing for you, I'm sure!'

These disjointed remarks were addressed to Mr. Valliscourt, who, alternately flushing and paling, under the influence of his mingled sensations of indignation at the dishonour wrought upon him by his wife, and vexation at the sudden illness of his son, presented a somewhat singular spectacle. Lionel had been brought into the house in a dead faint in the arms of a – a person – a common person, who sold eggs and butter and milk in the village and called herself Clarinda Cleverly Payne – what ridiculous names these Devonshire people gave themselves, to be sure! – and the – the person had presumed to express sympathy for him – for *him*, John Valliscourt of Valliscourt! – in his 'great misfortune' – and had also dared to compassionate his son – yes – had actually, before certain of the servants, said 'May God help the poor dear little motherless lamb!' It was most offensive and intrusive on the part of the person who called herself Clarinda – and Mr. Valliscourt as soon as she departed, had given strict injunctions that she was never again to be admitted inside the premises on any pretext whatever. This done, he had sent for the principal doctor in Combmartin, who had attended the summons promptly, trotting rapidly to the house on a stout cob, which, when he alighted from its broad back, was handed over to the care of an equally stout boy, who turned up mysteriously from somewhere in the village, and appearing simultaneously with the doctor, seemed to have been groom-in-ordinary to the cob all his life. The stout boy had, by some unknown process, transferred the roundness and ruddiness of two prize Devonshire apples into his cheeks, and he had another Devonshire apple in his pocket, which he presently took out, cut with a clasp-knife, and divided into equal proportions between the cob and himself, to occupy the time spent by them both in waiting for the doctor outside Mr. Valliscourt's hall-door. The doctor meanwhile had successfully roused Lionel from the death-like swoon that had lasted till he came – and Lionel himself, breathing faintly and irregularly, had half-opened his eyes, and was vaguely trying to think where he was, and what had happened to him.

'Yes' – continued Dr. Hartley musingly, now lifting with delicate finger one of the boy's eyelids, and peering at the ball of the soft eye beneath it – 'I should certainly take him away as quickly as convenient to yourself — '

'It's not convenient to me at all' – said Mr. Valliscourt irritably – '*I* can't go anywhere with him – my time is fully occupied – and his lessons will be materially interfered with—'

'Humph!' and the doctor glanced him over from head to foot with considerable disfavour — 'Well – you must decide for yourself of course – but it is my duty as a medical man to inform you that if the boy is not moved at once, and given some change from his present surroundings, there is a danger of meningitis setting in. And his constitution does not appear to me sufficiently robust to withstand it. Lessons, just now, are entirely out of the question.'

Mr. Valliscourt frowned. He took a sudden and violent aversion to Dr. Hartley. He disliked and resented the expression of the shrewd blue eyes that gave him such a straight look of criticism and censure – and he felt that here was another 'semi-barbaric fool' like Willie Montrose, who had beliefs and sentiments. He coughed in a stately manner, and said stiffly –

'Perhaps I can persuade Professor Cadman-Gore – '

'Who is he?' asked the doctor abruptly, laying his big gentle hand on Lionel's brow, and smoothing back the curls that clustered there with the sauve soft touch of a woman. Mr. Valliscourt stared – then smiled, a superior smile at the ignorance of this village Galen.

'Professor Cadman-Gore,' he announced with laboured politeness – 'is one of our greatest thinkers and logicians. His fame is almost universal – I should have thought it had penetrated even to this part of the country – that is, among the more cultured inhabitants' – and he laid a slight emphasis on the word 'cultured' – 'He is the author of many valuable scientific works, and is an admirable trainer and cultivator of youth. As a rule he never undertakes the instruction of a boy so young as my son – but out of consideration for me, hearing that I had been compelled to dismiss, rather suddenly, an incompetent tutor, he very kindly accepted the task of my son's holiday tuition. It is possible he might be willing to accompany the boy for the change you advise – if indeed you consider such a change absolutely necessary – '

'I do, most decidedly' – said Dr. Hartley, filling a teaspoon with some reviving cordial, and gently placing it to Lionel's lips, while Lionel in his turn feeling all the time as if he were in a dream swallowed the mixture obediently – 'I don't say take him far – for he must on no account be over-fatigued. Clovelly would be a good place. Let him go there with his tutor, and scramble about as he likes. The sooner the better. Here he will only think and fret about his mother. In fact you'd better order a carriage and have him taken on as far as Ilfracombe this very afternoon – then, the rest of the way can be done by easy stages. The coach would be too jolty for him. You can't go with him yourself, you say?'

'Impossible!' and Mr. Valliscourt's mouth hardened into

a thin tight line, indicative of inward and closely repressed rage – 'I must go to town at once for a few days – I have to consult my – my lawyers.'

'Oh – ah! Yes – I see – I understand!' and the doctor gave a little nod of comprehension – 'Well, can I have a talk with the boy's tutor? I should like to explain a few points to him.'

'Certainly. He is in the schoolroom – permit me to show you the way there.'

'One moment!' and Dr. Hartley gave a keen glance round the small apartment in which they were. It was Lionel's bedroom, whither he had been carried in his swoon by the warm-hearted Clarinda Cleverly Payne. The window was shut – but the doctor threw it wide open. 'Plenty of fresh air, nourishing food, and rest' – he said – 'That's what the boy wants. And he must be amused – he mustn't be left alone. Send one of the servants up here to sit with him, till he's ready to start this afternoon.'

'Send Lucy!' murmured Lionel's faint voice from the bed.

'What's that, my little man?' inquired the doctor, bending over him – 'Send whom?'

'Lucy,' – and Lionel looked up fearlessly in his physician's round, shiny face – 'She is a housemaid, and a very nice girl. I like her.'

Dr. Hartley smiled. 'Very good! You shall have Lucy. The desirable young woman shall come up to you at once. Now, how do you feel?'

'Much better, thank you!' and the boy's eyes softened gratefully – 'But – you know . . . I can't – I can't forget things . . . not very easily!'

The doctor made no answer to this remark, but merely settled the pillows more comfortably under his small patient's head. Then he went away with Mr. Valliscourt to make the acquaintance of Professor Cadman-Gore. And when Lucy came creeping softly up, as commanded, to watch by Lionel's bedside, she found the little fellow sleeping, with traces of tears glistening on his pale cheeks; and his aspect was so touching and solemn in its innocence and sorrow and helplessness, that being nothing but a woman and a warm-hearted woman too, she took out her handkerchief and had a good quiet cry all to herself. 'How could she – how *could* she leave the little dear!' she wondered dolefully, as she thought of the reckless and shameful flight of her recent mistress – 'To leave *him*' – meaning Mr. Valliscourt – 'isn't so surprising, howsumever it's wicked, for he's a handful to live with and no mistake! – but to leave her own boy – that's real downright bad of her! – that it is!'

Poor Lucy! She had never read the works of Ibsen, and was entirely ignorant of the 'New Morality.' Had she been taught these modern ethics, she would have recognised in Mrs. Valliscourt's conduct merely a 'noble' outbreak of 'white purity' and virtue. But she had 'barbaric' notions of motherhood – she believed in its sacredness in quite an obstinate, prejudiced and old-fashioned way. She was nothing but a 'child of nature,' poor, simple Ibsen-less housemaid Lucy! – and throughout all creation, nature makes mother-love a law, and mother's duty paramount.

Meanwhile Dr. Hartley had the stupendous honour of shaking hands with Professor Cadman-Gore – and not only did he seem totally unimpressed by the occurrence, but he had actually the sublime impudence to ask for a private interview with the great man – that is, an interview without the presence of Mr. Valliscourt. The latter personage, surprised and somewhat offended, reluctantly left the two gentlemen together for the space of about fifteen minutes – at the end of which time the Professor looked more ponderously thoughtful than usual, and Dr. Hartley took his leave, trotting off on his stout cob amid many respectful salutations from the stout boy, who straightway disappeared also, to those unknown regions of Combmartin whence he had emerged, as if by magic, directly his services were required.

And Lionel slept on and on, till, at a little after three o'clock in the afternoon, Lucy roused him and gave him a cup of soup, which seemed to him particularly strong and well-flavoured.

'There's wine in it, isn't there?' he asked, with a surprised glance, whereat Lucy nodded smiling. 'Fancy giving me wine in my soup! Oh, I say! It's too good for me!'

Lucy gave a slight sniff, and stated she had a cold.

'It's my belief that this old house is damp' – she said – 'And the whole village is crazy-built and green-mouldy in my opinion! And what do you think, Master Lionel? If that blessed old "Hoddy-Doddy," the silly man you saw the other morning, ain't been here shaking his wobbly head over the gate and giving all his roses in for you, for nothing! And here they are!' and she raised a beautiful cluster of deep red, pale pink, and white half-open buds, fragrant and dewy – 'We couldn't make out what he wanted at first, he was so wobbly and couldn't speak plain – but at last we got at it – it was "For the little boy – the little boy" – over and over again. So we took the flowers just to please the poor creature – he wouldn't have any money for them. He saw you being carried home in your faint by Miss Payne, and he thought you were dead.'

'Did he?' murmured Lionel wistfully – 'And that is why he brought the flowers I suppose – thinking me dead! Poor man! He's very dreadful to look at – but he's very kind I daresay – and he can't help his looks, can he?'

'No, that he can't,' – agreed Lucy simply – 'And after all, it's what we are that God cares about, not what we seem to be.'

At these words a deep sadness clouded the boy's eyes, and he thought of his mother. Was there a God to care what became of *her*? Or was there only the Atom, to whom nothing mattered, neither sin, nor sorrow, nor death? Oh, if he could only be sure that it was really a God who was the Supreme Cause and Mover of all things – a wise, loving, pitiful, forgiving, Eternal and Divine Being, how he would pray to Him for his lost, unhappy, beautiful mother, and ask Him to bring her back! But he had no time to ponder on such questions, for Lucy was now busy putting on his overcoat, and finding his hat, and packing his little valise, and doing all sorts of things – and while he was yet wondering at these arrangements, and trying to stand firmly on his legs, which were curiously weak and shaky, who should come striding largely across the threshold of his bedroom, but Professor Cadman-Gore! Professor Cadman-Gore, with broad soft wide-awake on, and extensive flapping over-all – his habitual costume when travelling, even in the hottest weather – and more wonderful than the wide-awake or the over-all, was the smile that wrinkled the Professor's grim features in several new places, making little unaccustomed lines of agreeable suggestiveness among the deeper furrows of thought, and even turning up the stiff corners of his mouth in quite a strange manner, inasmuch as his usual sort of smile always turned those corners down. 'Hullo!' said the learned man, with a sprightly air – 'How are you now?'

'Better, thank you!' answered Lionel, gently – 'My head is a little swimmy, that's all.'

'Oh, that's all, is it? Well, that isn't much!' and the Professor stood alternatively glowering and grinning, with a distinctly evident desire to make himself agreeable – 'Can you ride pick-a-back?'

Lionel stared wonderingly – then smiled.

'Why, yes! I haven't often done it – but I know how!'

'Come along then!' and the Professor squatted down and bent his bony shoulders to the necessary level – 'I'll take you to the carriage that way. Hold on tight!'

Lionel was stricken quite speechless with sheer amazement. What! Professor Cadman-Gore, the great scholar, the not-to-be-contradicted logician, condescending to carry a boy pick-a-back! Such a thing was astounding – unheard-of! Surely it ought to be chronicled in the newspapers under a bold head-line thus –

GRACIOUS CONDUCT OF AN OXFORD PROFESSOR.

'Do you mean it? Really?' he asked timidly, flushing with surprise.

'Certainly I do! Only don't keep me waiting long in this – this absurd attitude!' And ferocity and kindness together played at such cross-purposes on his lantern-jawed visage, that Lionel lost no time in getting his little legs astride round the sinewy neck of the distinguished man, trembling as he did so at the very idea of taking such a liberty with a walking encyclopaedia of wisdom. And downstairs they went, master and pupil in this wondrous fashion, to the hall-door, outside which there was a big landau and a pair of sleek brown horses waiting, and where Lionel was slipped easily off the Professor's back into a pile of soft cushions and covered up with warm rugs. Then Lucy bustled about, packing all manner of odds and ends into the carriage, and openly flirting with the coach-man in the very presence of the great Cadman-Gore – one or two of the other servants came out to look and wave their hands – then the horses started – Lucy called, 'Good-bye, Master Lionel! Come back quite well!' and away they drove through the beautiful sunshiny air, down the one principal street of Combmartin, past the quiet little harbour, and up the picturesque road leading to Ilfracombe. Mr. Valliscourt had not appeared to bid his little son good-bye – and Lionel though he noticed the fact, did not regret it. Resting comfort-ably among his pillows he was very silent, though now and then he stole a furtive glance at the Professor, who sat bolt upright, surveying the landscape through his spectacles with the severely critical air of a man who knows just how scenery is made, and won't stand any nonsense about it – and it was not till they had left Combmartin some distance behind them that he ventured to ask gently –

'Where are we going?'

'To Clovelly,' replied the Professor, bringing his owl-like glasses to bear on the little wistful face upturned to him – 'But not tonight. We only get as far as Ilfracombe this afternoon.'

'Is my father coming?'

'No. He's going to London on business. He'll be away a week or ten days, and so shall we. Then we shall return to Combmartin, and stay there till your father's summer tenancy of the house expires.'

'I see!' murmured Lionel – 'I understand!' And two great tears filled his eyes. He was thinking of his mother. But her name never passed his lips. He turned his face a little away, and thought he had hidden his emotions from his tutor – but he thought wrongly, for the Professor had seen the gleam of those unfalling tears, and, strange to say, was moved thereby to what was for him a most unusual sentiment of pity. He, who had frequently witnessed the ruthless vivisection of innocent animals – he, who had tranquilly watched a poor butterfly writhe itself to death on his scientific pin, was at last touched in the innermost recesses of his heart by the troubles of a child. And so perchance, he established a claim for himself in the heaven he so strenuously denied – a claim that might possibly be of more avail to him in the Great Hereafter than all his book-learning and world-logic.

Meanwhile, John Valliscourt of Valliscourt, shut up in his own room in the now lonely house at Combmartin, wrote to his lawyers preparing them for his visit to their office the next day, and instructed them at once to sue for his divorce from Helen Valliscourt, the co-respondent in the case being Charles Lascelles, Baronet. There would be no defence, he added – and then, turning from his own methodical statement of the facts, he took up and re-read the letter his recreant wife had written him by way of farewell. It ran thus –

'I leave you without shame, and without remorse. While I was faithful to you, you made my life a misery. Your pride and egotism need humbling – I am glad to be at last the means of dragging you down in the dust of dishonour. You have killed every womanly sentiment in me – you have even separated me from my child. You have robbed me of God, of hope, of every sense of duty. I have gone with Charles Lascelles, whose chief merit in my eyes is that he hates you as much as I do! In other respects you know his character, and so do I. When you divorce me, he will not marry me – I would not have him if he offered. I have consented to be his mistress in exchange for a year's amusement, attention and liberty – and for the rest of my life what shall I do? I neither know, nor care! Perhaps I shall repent – perhaps I shall die. To me nothing matters – your creed – the creed of Self – suffices. Your Self is content with dull respectability – my Self craves indulgence. If anything could have kept me straight, and given me patience to bear with your arrogance and pedantry, it would have been my boy's love, but that you are deliberately bent on depriving me of. Every day you set up new barriers between him and me. And yet I loved you once – *you !* – I laugh now to think of my folly! You did everything you could to crush that love out of me – you have succeeded! What remnant of a heart I have, is left with Lionel – my spirit is in the boy's blood, and already he rebels against your petty tyranny. Sooner or later he will escape you – may it be soon for the poor child's own sake! – and then – whether there be a God or no God, you will reap the curses you have so lavishly sown! May they amply reward you for your "generosity" to

'Your wife no longer,
'Helen.'

Over and over again Mr. Valliscourt read these words, till

they seemed burned into his brain – far into the night he mused upon their purport – and the phrases 'My spirit is in the boy's blood,' 'already he rebels' – 'sooner or later he will escape you', sounded loudly in his ears, like threats from some unseen enemy.

'No!' he muttered, rising from his chair at last, and thrusting the letter into a secret drawer of his desk – 'Let her go, the jade! – the way of all such trash! – let her mix herself with the mud of the street and be forgotten – but the boy is mine! he shall obey me – and I will crush her spirit out of him, and make of him what I choose!'

CHAPTER 12

Poor Clovelly – beautiful Clovelly! Once an ideal village for poets to sing of, and artists to dream of, to what 'base uses' hast thou come! Now no longer a secluded bower for the 'melancholy mild-eyed lotus-eaters' of thought – no longer a blessed haven of rest for weary souls seeking cessation from care and toil, thou art branded as a 'place of interest' for cheap trippers, who with loud noise of scrambling feet, and goose-like gigglings, crowd thy one lovely upward-winding street – which is like nothing so much as a careless garland of flowers left by chance on the side of a hill – and thrust their unromantic figures and vulgarly inquisitive faces through thy picturesque doorways and quaint fuchsia-wreathed lattice-windows. It is as though a herd of swine should suddenly infest a fairy's garden, nosing the fine elfin air, and rooting up the magic blossoms. Demoralised Clovelly! Even thy inhabitants, originally simple-hearted, gentle, and hospitable with all the unaffected primitive sweetness of oldest English hospitality, are tainted by the metropolitan disease of money-grubbing – love of 'the chinks' is fast superseding the love of nature, though Nature herself, with many fond tears of appealing love, still twines the jessamine and pushes the may-blossom over the roofs and against the walls of the cherished spot, and pleads in all her tenderest ways for its preservation. 'Leave Clovelly to me!' she cries – 'Let the tramping herd wander over the face of foreign lands if they must and will – let them break their soda-water bottles against the ruins of the Colosseum in Rome – let them write their worthless names on the topmost statue adorning Milan Cathedral – let them paint their glaring advertisements across the rocks and glaciers of Switzerland –

let them chip at the features of the Sphinx, and scrawl vile phrases on the Pyramids – but spare me Clovelly! Let me still keep the guardianship of my own sea-paradise – let me twist the crimson fuchsia round the doors, and bunch the purple blossoms of wistaria above the windows – let me grow my daisies and bright pimpernels in the crannies of the climbing street – let me trail the golden "creeping Jenny" down the stone steps of side dwellings and in quaint hole-and-corner alleys – let me wreath the honeysuckle in fragrant tufts about the balconies and chimneys, and let me put all the sweetness of my flowers, my sea-foam, my bright air, and my fresh foliage into the hearts of the people! I would fain keep them a race apart – the women simple, noble, maternal – the men strong, brave, God-fearing and manly, with eyes grown blue in the fronting of the sea, and hearts kept young by the companionship of flowers and children – so that even when storm rushes in from the Atlantic and makes of my Clovelly nothing but a shining gleam of light in a haze of rain, and the thunder of the billows on the shore is as God's voice arguing with His creation, these village-folk may be unafraid and calm, with faith in their souls and love in their hearts, a contrast to the dwellers in cities, who, pampered and spoilt in their fancied security of wealth and ease, cower and scurry away from the slightest touch of misfortune as rats fly from a falling house! Release me from the scourge of savages and pilferers who have thrust themselves in upon this my deeply-hidden nook and favourite bower! – let me keep Clovelly "unspotted from the world"!'

Thus Nature; – but her appeal is vain. She could not save Foyers – she will not save Clovelly. The spoiler's hand has fallen – the work of destruction has already begun, not outwardly, but inwardly. What though the present owners of the land have vowed to keep Clovelly as it is – what though they rightly and justly refuse to have hotels built, and lodging-houses set up, to deface one of the most unique and exquisite spots in all creation? The taint is in the hearts of the people – the love of gain – the greed of cash; discontent and ambition, like two evil genii, have crept into Fairyland, and their prompt- ings and suggestions will in time prevail more strongly than all the earnest voices of good angels!

Lionel led a curious sort of life at Clovelly. He and the Professor occupied the quaintest and funniest little rooms that were ever designed – rooms with floors that sloped and ceilings that slanted, and that altogether suggested the remains of some earthquake, by reason of numerous wide cracks in the walls and gaps in the chimney-nooks, and that yet were pretty with an odd, old-world prettiness not found everywhere. The landlady of these 'desirable apartments' was a bakeress by profession, though she did many other useful things besides baking bread and letting lodgings. She was a clean, buxom- looking woman and had excellent notions concerning the wholesomeness of fresh air and sweet linen – so that all her beds were lavender-scented, and her entire abode neatly ordered, and redolent of the honeysuckle and the roses that clambered round her windows. She was unceasing in her care for her lodgers – her anxious deference towards the grim- featured long-legged Professor knew no bounds, while her warm heart was quite taken captive by the plaintive gentleness and pretty ways of Lionel, whom she always called 'the dear little boy' – a term which set Lionel himself thinking. Was he so very little? He was nearly eleven – surely that was almost a man! True, his mother had called him her 'baby' – and his inwardly-grieving soul suffered an additional pang at his recollection of her tenderness. He dared not dwell upon the image of her face as it had looked in the white moonlight, when she kissed him for the last time – was it indeed the last time, he wondered sadly? – should he ever see her again?

He had full leisure now for thought – the Professor let him wander about just as he liked, and was altogether extraordin- arily kind to him. He could not quite make it out – but he was grateful. And he used to show his gratitude in odd little ways of his own, which had a curious and softening effect on the mind of the learned Cadman-Gore. He would carefully brush the ugly hat of the great man and bring it to him – he would pull out and smooth the large sticky fingers of his loose leather gloves, and lay them side by side on a table ready for him to wear – he would energetically polish the top of his big silver-knobbed stick – and he would invariably make a 'button-hole' of the prettiest flowers he could find, for him to put in his coat at dinner. The astonishment with which the distinguished disciplinarian first received these attentions, and afterwards grew to expect them every day as a matter of course, was something remarkable. And it is to be noted that the worthy Cadman-Gore was so far removed from his usual self during these sunshiny days at Clovelly, as to go rummaging down, down, into the far recesses of his own past youth, and search there for fragments of fairy-tales, which fragments, laid hold of after much difficulty, he would piece together laboriously for Lionel's benefit and amusement.

One day it occurred to him that he would relate in 'fairy' style, the beautiful old classic legend of Cupid and Psyche, and see what the boy made of it. They had gone for a walk that afternoon along the 'Hobby Drive,' and had paused to sit down and rest on a grassy knoll from which the sea gleamed distantly, like a turquoise set in diamonds, between the tremulous foliage of the bending trees. And in his harsh hoarse voice which he vainly strove to soften, the Professor told the tender and poetic story – of the happiness of Psyche with her divine lover, till that fatal night, when she held her little lamp aloft that she might satisfy her curiosity, and see for herself the actual shape and lineaments of the god – then came the thunder and the darkness – the breaking and extinguishing of the lamp – the rush of great wings through the midnight – and lo, Love had fled – and poor Psyche was left alone weeping. And ever since, has she not been solitary? – searching for the vanished Glory which she knows of, yet cannot find? Lionel listened in rapt silence, his earnest eyes every now and then raised to his tutor's furrowed visage, which under the influence of the beauty of Clovelly, and the wistful presence of the child, had taken upon itself a certain expression of benevolence that struggled to overcome and banish the old long lines of practised austerity.

'I like that story' – he said, when it was finished, 'And I see a lot of meaning in it – quite serious meaning, you know! May I tell you what I think about it?'

Professor Cadman-Gore nodded. Lionel, taking up the large wide-awake hat that lay on the grass, proceeded to delicately remove without injury, a tiny grasshopper that had boldly presumed to settle on that misshapen covering of one of the wisest heads in Christendom.

'You see Psyche didn't know, and she wanted to find out,' he went on, musingly – 'That's just like me, and you, and everybody, isn't it? And then we light our little lamps and begin to try to discover things – and perhaps we think we have found the Atom – when all at once, the thunder comes and the darkness – and we die! – our lamps go out! But we don't hear the rush of wings, do we? If we only heard that – just the rush of wings – we should feel that Someone had gone – Somewhere! – and we should try to follow – I'm sure we should try. Perhaps we shall hear it when we die – that rush of wings – and we shall know what we can't know now, because our lamps go out so quickly.'

The Professor was silent. He could find nothing to say, inasmuch as there was no contradiction to offer to the boy's logic. Lionel meanwhile doubled one leg loosely under him on the grass, and throwing off his cap, let the light flower-scented wind play with his fair curly locks.

'Now for people who believe in Christ' – he continued – 'There it is – that rush of wings – because they say "He rose from the dead and ascended into Heaven." And they have just that feeling I suppose – that Someone has gone Somewhere, and they try to follow it as best they can. That's how it is, I am sure, and it must be a great help to them. I should dearly like to believe some of the beautiful things in the Bible. In old Genesis, for instance, you know if there were a God, it would be quite natural that when He made a place like Clovelly, He should be pleased. And then those words would be exactly right – "And God saw all that He had made, and behold it was very good!" '

Professor Cadman-Gore's love of argument stirred rebelliously in him, but he gave it no speech. He would have liked to say that there were a great many learned persons who, thinking that they saw all that God had made, said 'behold, it was very bad!' Humane persons too, who, unable to look behind the veil, could not understand the reason of the stress and worry, and torture of life; but to this little, frail, sorrowstricken lad, but lately tottering on the verge of a dangerous illness, he could not propound any problems, so he was mercifully silent. Once a thought leaped across his brain like a blinding flash of light, startling him with its acute shock – and it was this; – *'What a monstrous crime it is to bring up this child without a faith!'* Amazed at his own involuntary and unusual feeling, he resolutely crushed it back into the innermost depths of his consciousness – yet every now and then it would persistently recur to him, accompanied by other thoughts of a like nature which worried him, and which he had never dwelt upon with so much pertinacity before. A teasing inward voice asked him questions, such as – 'Was it right to attack, and endeavour to pull down Faith, when nothing, could be offered in place of it?' For Faith, substitute Reason, argued the Professor. 'But,' went on the voice, 'Reason is apt to totter on its throne. Grief will subdue it – Passion overcome it. The ecstasy of love will hurl its votaries beyond all the bounds of sense or arguments – into folly, sin, desperation, death! The madness and abandonment of grief will make of the miserable human thing a mere despairing clamour – a figure of frenzy with wild hair and piteous eyes – what can Reason do with such? Only Faith can save – faith in a God of Love; and the words – "*Whoso shall offend one of these little ones which believe in Me, it were better for him that a millstone were hanged about his neck, and that he were drowned in the depths of the sea*" must rest for ever as a curse upon every man or woman who by word, deed or example, strives to tear down the one divine support of struggling souls – the one great prop of a world contending with ceaseless storm.' So murmured the inward voice; and hearing it discourse thus plainly, the Professor, thought his intellectual faculties must be decaying. Something strange was at work within him – something to which he could not give a name – something which perchance would make of him in time a wiser man than he had yet assumed himself to be.

During this peaceful and absolutely idle holiday at Clovelly, Lionel used often to go down the winding way from the village to the rough cobbly beach, and sit and talk to the boatmen gathered there. They liked the little lad, and would frequently take him out in their fishing-smacks for a toss on the sea, though from these excursions he did not return much the brighter, but rather the sadder. The Clovelly men have many a harrowing tale to tell of shipwreck, and of poor drowned creatures washed ashore with eyes staring open to the pitiless sky, and hands clinging convulsively to a bit of rope or spar – and such narratives as these they would relate to the boy in their own roughly eloquent, realistic way, till his heart grew cold within him, and he almost learned to hate the sea. The old weary wonder came back to his brain and tortured him – what was the good of it all? What was the use of living or loving, hoping or working? None, that he could see!

On one rather stormy afternoon towards sunset, he was strolling as usual down to the beach, when he was attracted by a little crowd of men that stood closely grouped round the door of an open boat-house. They were all peering in with an expression of mingled horror and morbid fascination in their faces, and as he came near, one of them motioned him to stand back.

'What's the matter?' he asked anxiously – 'Is some one drowned?'

'No, no, little measter,' – answered a tough old seaman standing by. 'The sea's not to blame this time. But it's no sight for you – it's a stranger to us, a sort o' queer tourist-like chap – he's bin an' hanged hisself in Davey Loame's boat-house.'

'Hanged himself!' cried Lionel, horrified – 'Why, how could he do that?'

'Easy, enough – nothin' easier if ye've got a neckercher an' a nail. An' he had both. He made a loop wi' 's neckercher an' swung on to an iron hook in the roof. They've cut him down, but he's stone dead – 'tain't no use tryin' to revive him. We don't know who he is, anyway. But you go right home, little measter – 'tain't the thing for you to be here – now run along just like the good boy y' are. It's too rough to take y' out sailin' to-day.'

Lionel felt a strange sickness at his heart, as he turned away obediently, and began to climb the ascent towards the village. His vivid imagination pictured the dreadful, strange dead body found in the boat-house – and involuntarily he paused and looked back over his shoulder out to sea. Great billows rolling in from the Atlantic were racing shorewards, crested with foam – the long lines of snaky-white intermingled and wove themselves together, like a glittering net spread out to catch and drown poor helpless men. The impression of the universal Cruelty of things, weighed on the boy's mind with renewed force, and at his evening meal he looked so pale and weary, that Professor Cadman-Gore, glowering anxiously at him through his round spectacles, asked him what was the matter? Lionel could not very well explain – but at last, after some hesitation, said he thought it was the hanged man that made him feel miserable.

'What hanged man?' inquired the startled Professor.

Whereupon Lionel related all that he knew concerning the disagreeable incident, and the worthy Cadman-Gore was somewhat relieved. He had thought that perhaps his young pupil had been allowed to see the body, and was glad to learn that this was not the case.

'Oh well, hanging is a very easy death,' he said, placidly – 'Quite painless and merciful. I daresay the man was some tramp who had no money, and didn't know where to get any.'

'But isn't that very, very dreadful?' asked Lionel, 'Isn't it cruel that a poor man should not be able to find one friend in the whole world to save him from hanging himself?'

'It seems cruel,' admitted the Professor gently – he was always gentle with Lionel now – 'But, after all, who knows! Death is not the worst evil – we must all die – and there are some people who wish to die before their time, and who would be very sorry if they were hindered in making the "happy dispatch." The Chinese and Japanese, as you have read in some of your books, attach no importance to the act of dying, and with them, suicide is often considered honourable. This particular man had the means of death at hand – a necker-chief and a strong nail, – and that's all he wanted I suppose. It was rather selfish of him though to use another man's boat-house for the purpose, when he could have done it just as well by throwing himself into the sea.'

Lionel said no more on the subject – nor did he make inquiries in the village respecting the 'Unknown case of suicide' which was presently chronicled in all the Devon newspapers. But the incident had a considerable effect upon him, and remained a fixture in his memory, all the more pertinaciously that he was silent concerning it.

They returned at last to Combmartin, after having stayed at Clovelly nearly a fortnight. Lionel was looking, on the whole, much better for the rest and change, though his face was still thin and colourless. The sad expression of his eyes had not altered, nor had the inward sorrow of his heart for his mother's loss abated, – but a kind of passive resignation, mingled with hope, now possessed and tranquillised him, and he had secretly determined to try and get on extra fast with his studies, and grow up quickly so that as soon as he became a man, he might seek his mother out wherever she was, and persuade her to come back to him. Of her faults or her shame he never thought, – she was his mother, – and that was enough for him. He said something about his intention of studying hard to the Professor, as they drove along the lovely Devonshire lanes on their homeward way, – but that gentleman did not seem to take up the matter very enthusiastically.

'Certainly,' he said, 'you can continue a few of your studies if you like, – but you must not resume the whole course at once. To-morrow morning for instance, you can go for a ramble just as you have been doing at Clovelly, and if you feel inclined to take a book with you, why do so by all means. But as you have been ill, we must not commence work in too much of a hurry, or we shall have the doctor coming round again.'

He produced his new smile – the smile he had been cultivating with such success during the past twelve days – and Lionel smiled gratefully in response. A happy thought flashed across the boy's mind – as he was to enjoy the freedom of a 'ramble' all to himself the next morning, he would go and see Jessamine Dale. How pleased she would be! – how surprised! – how her beautiful little face would dimple all over with mischievous and winsome smiles! – how her sweet blue eyes would shine and sparkle! A quiver of delight and expectancy ran through him and sent colour to his cheeks, and as the carriage rattled up the Combmartin street and turned into the familiar avenue leading up to the house he at present called home, he felt almost happy. His father had returned from London, and received him with chilly dignity.

'I am glad to see you looking so robust, Lionel,' – he said, as he touched his son's tremblingly-offered little hand – then turning to Professor Cadman-Gore, he added – 'I trust, Professor, your patience has not been too severely tried?'

The Professor looked at him with quite a whimsical air.

'Well, to tell you the truth, Valliscourt, it hasn't been tried at all!' he answered – 'I've enjoyed myself very much, and that's a fact. Clovelly's a charming place, and the people are interesting, as being just in the transition-stage between primitive simplicity and modern cupidity. There are rather too many tourists and amateur photographers – but one can't have everything one's own way, in this world – even *you* must have found that out occasionally.'

Mr. Valliscourt's smooth brow reddened slightly. He had indeed 'found that out' to his cost; but he had yet to discover that even so far as the Theory of Atoms went, the human atom was bound to follow the course of the Divine one, or else get into a strangely contrary path of its own, ending in darkness and disaster. For the universe is composed as a perfect harmony – and if one note sounds a discord, it is sooner or later invariably silenced. Every instrument must be in tune to play the great Symphony well – otherwise there is a clashing of elements, a casting out of unworthy performers, and a new beginning.

CHAPTER 13

NEXT day the weather was warm and sunny – and when Lionel formally applied to his tutor for permission to go and enjoy the already promised 'ramble', it was at once granted. Being a conscientious little fellow, he voluntarily suggested taking his Latin grammar with him, but the Professor did not encourage him in this idea.

'No,' he said – 'As I told you yesterday, you can amuse yourself as you like this morning – tomorrow, perhaps we will resume the lessons.'

With a bright smile and flashing eye, Lionel thanked him, and quickly putting on his cap, he hastened out of the school-room, down the stairs, and into the garden. He was quite light-hearted – indeed he felt almost ashamed to be so glad. Life had not changed for him just because the sun was shining and the birds were singing, and he was going to see little Jessamine Dale! Things remained exactly as they were – he was nothing but a lonely boy whose mother had wilfully deserted him – had he forgotten that misery and her disgrace so soon? No – he had not forgotten; his was a nature that could never forget; but youth is youth, and will, in its own season, have its way despite all sorrow and restraint – and somehow on this beautiful bright morning he could not feel sad. There was something radiant and hopeful in the aspect of the very landscape, green with leafage and golden with ripe corn – and as he swung open his father's carriage-gate and went out along the high-road towards the grey and ancient church of Combmartin, where he thought it was most likely he should find Reuben Dale, and Jessamine also, he was quietly happy. All sorts of plans were forming in his little head – he was beginning to like Professor Cadman-Gore, and he meant to ask him if he might not go on studying under him, at his (the Professor's) own house for a time, before entering a public school – that is, if he were indeed intended to enter a public school – of which he was always doubtful. True, his father had once *said* 'Winchester' – but whether he *meant* Winchester, was quite another matter. Mr. Montrose had urged sending him to a public school, and Mr. Valliscourt had curtly negativ-ed the proposal entirely. Lionel's own opinion was that his education would always be carried on under a series of selected tutors, in order to avoid the conventional 'church-going' on Sundays common to all schools, and to which his father had such a rooted and obstinate objection. And as, according to all accounts, no wiser man than Professor Cadman-Gore existed, why should he not remain with that head and fount of all available knowledge? He thought his father could not possibly raise any obstacle to such a scheme; – 'and then', he reflected – 'though even the Professor can't tell me what I want to know about the Atom, he might put me gradually in the way of finding that out for myself. I believe he really likes me a little now – I suppose we got to know each other better at Clovelly. At any rate, for all his queer looks, he understands me more than my father does. It is very difficult for a boy to be understood by old people, I think. I'm sure a great many boys never get understood at all, and yet they have their ideas about things quite as much as grown-up persons do. How pretty the church looks with all that sunshine streaming on the old tower! – and there's Mr. Dale! – digging a grave as usual!'

With a smile he quickened his pace to a run, and, opening the churchyard gate, went in quickly but noiselessly, meaning to take Jessamine by surprise if she were anywhere near. Treading lightly and almost on tiptoe, he came to within about an arm's length of Reuben Dale without the latter perceiving him, and then stopped short – struck by a sudden alarm. For Reuben's silvery head was bent low and heavily over his work –

and from Reuben's broad breast came great choking sobs, terrible to hear, as one by one the spadefuls of red-brown earth were thrown up on the green turf, and the significant hollow in the ground was shaped slowly in a small dark square, to the length of a little child. A mist rose before Lionel's eyes – a strange contraction caught his throat with a sense of suffocation – he advanced tremblingly, his hands outstretched.

'Mr. Dale!' – he faltered, 'Oh – Mr. Dale . . .'

Reuben looked up – great tears were rolling down his face – and for a moment he said nothing. The dreadful, inarticulate despair expressed in his features and attitude was harrowing to behold; – and Lionel felt as though an icy hand had suddenly clutched his heart and stilled its beating. Fear held him speechless – he could only wait in breathless terror for something to be told – something he could not guess at, but which instinctively he dreaded to hear. And all at once Reuben spoke, in hoarse tremulous accents:

'She sent her love t'ye my dear – she sent her love – 'twos the last thing – "my love to Lylie," – I wosn't to forgit it – the blessed little angel-smile she had too in sayin' it, my Jess'mine flower! – "my love to Lylie!" they wos her last words, a minit 'fore she died.'

'Died!' gasped Lionel, a horrible tremor shaking his limbs – 'Died! – Jessamine? . . . Jessamine *dead*? No, no, *no*! It's not possible – it can't be! – you know it can't – you're dreaming . . . it can't be true! . . .'

A loud noise wos in his ears like the rushing of waters – the haze that hung before his eyes turned a dull red – and with a sudden wild scream he sprang to Reuben like some poor little hunted, frantic animal, clinging to him, hiding his head against him, and gripping his arms convulsively.

'No – no! – not dead. Don't say it! – not little Jessamine! Oh, you're not – you're not going to put her down there in the cold earth! – not little Jessamine! Oh, hold me! – I'm frightened – I am indeed! I can't bear it – I can't, I can't! – oh Jessamine! . . . she isn't dead – not really ! – oh, do say she isn't – it would be too wicked – too cruel! . . .'

Reuben Dale, startled out of his own grief by the boy's terrible frenzy, let his spade fall, and held the little fellow tenderly in his arms, close to his breast, and with a strong effort, strove himself to be calm, in order to soothe the younger sufferer.

'Didn't ye hear of it, my dear?' he murmured, in low, broken tones – 'But no – I forgot – ye wouldn't hear – ye've bin away a goodish bit; – I heerd as how ye'd bin ill an' taken to Clovelly – an' 'twosn't likely any folks would tell ye of just a poor man's trouble. I went down yon to your feyther's house to tell ye – for Jessamine wos iver talkin' of ye, whensoever the fever in her little throat would let her speak – an' that's how I heerd ye were gone. 'Twos the diphtheria the darlin' caught – it's bin bad about the village – an' 'twos onny a matter o' fower days that she suffered. An' we did all we could for the lamb – an' Dr. Hartley, God bless i'm, wos wi' her day an' night, an' scarcely breaking fast, the good man that he is – an' I do b'lieve he'd 'a' laid down his own life to save 'er, as I'd 'a' laid down mine. But 'twos all no use – she was just too sweet a blossom to be spared to the likes of us, my lad – an' – an' so God took 'er as it's right an' just He should do what He wills wi' 's own – but oh, my lad, it's powerful 'ard on me, who am a weak an' a selfish sinner at best – it's powerful 'ard! First the mother – then the child! – Lord, give me strength to say "Thy will be done," for my own force as a man is gone out o' me, an' I'm but a broken reed in a rough wind!'

His head drooped forlornly over the boy he held clasped in his arms, and who still clung nervously to him, shaking like an aspen leaf and moaning querulously, as though in physical pain. The blue sky above them was clear of all clouds, and the sun shone royally, pouring down its golden beams into the little unfinished grave, like a ray of light from some left-open gate of Paradise. Suddenly, and with a pale horror imprinted on his countenance that made it look older by a dozen years, Lionel lifted himself and turned slowly round – his eyes were dry and feverishly bright – his forehead puckered like that of some aged man.

'You are going to put her down there?' he whispered fearfully, pointing to the grave – 'Little Jessamine? You are going to cover up her beautiful curls and blue eyes in all that red-brown earth? How can you have the heart to do it! – oh, how can you! She used to laugh and play – she will never laugh or play any more – you will hide her down there for ever – for ever!' and his voice rose to a wail of agony – 'We shall never see her again – never! – oh, Jessamine! – Jessamine!'

The stricken Reuben, pierced to the very soul by this wild grief in which he had the greatest share, knew of no other consolation save that which he derived from his simple and steadfast faith in God; but this supported him when otherwise he would have altogether broken down. Gently stroking the boy's curls with one big, work-worn hand, he murmured pityingly:

'Poor lad, poor lad! She wos fond of ye – she sent ye her love at the last – ye must think o' that, my dear. An' once when the pain was better, an' she could speak clear, she said, "Tell Lylie I'll see 'im soon – long 'fore he grows up to be a big man." Them wos her very words, the darlin', but she wos a-ramblin' like, an' didn't know wot she was a-talkin' of. She died easy – bless the Lord for all His mercies! – night afore last she put her arms out to me an' said "Dada!" quite bright like – that wos how she called me when she wos a babby – then, smilin' – "My love to Lylie," an' just went off quiet. An' there she lies in her little coffin, wi' a wreath o' jess'mine round her hair, an' a posy o' jess'mine in her wee hands – ay, we ha' pulled all the jess'mine flowers off the tree at our

172

door to put wi' her; – we want none o' them for our sad selves – now!'

A rising sob choked his brave utterance – but Lionel was still dry-eyed, and now moving restlessly, withdrew from the kind embrace which had supported him. Stumbling giddily forward a step or two, he fell on his knees beside the dark little square in the ground.

'Down there!' he whispered hoarsely, peering into the very depths of the gave – 'Down there! – Jessamine!'

He gave a convulsive gesture with his hands, clasping and unclasping them nervously and prying still with an intense, passionate searching horror into the dank mould. Reuben's touch, light and caressing as a woman's, fell gently on his shoulder.

'Nay, my little lad!' he said, the tears in his voice shaking its deep tone to tenderest pathos – 'Not down there! – don't ye think it! Up there, my dear, up there!' and he raised his steadfast eyes to the perfect blue of the radiant heaven – 'Up there, beyond all that summer light an' shinin' glory – in the land o' God an' His holy angels – that's where Jess'mine is now! "With Christ, which is far better!" Ay, my dear, far better! For it's onny my selfish heart which grudges her to God – it's just *me*, a weak, ignorant man, wot can't see the Lord's meanin' in takin' her from me; but surely He knows best – He *must* know best. An' mebbe He has seen the darlin' wosn't fitted for the hard an' thorny ways o' life – an' so in very kindness has took her to Himself, an' made of her an angel 'fore her time. For angel she is now ye may be sure – as innocent as ever stood afore the Great White Throne – an' it's not Jess'mine I'm laying down here among the daisies, my lad, but just the little earthly shape of her, wot wos s' pretty an' light an' gamesome like – we couldn't choose but love it, all of us – but Jess'mine herself is livin' yet – yes, my dear, livin' an' lovin' o' me as much an' more than ever she did – an' there's naught shall come atween us now. Mother an' child

173

are wi' the Lord – an' in a matter o' short years I'll meet them both again an' know as how 'twos for the best; though now it seems a mystery, an' partin's hard!'

Lionel looked up – his face was ashen pale – his lips were set in a thin vindictive line.

'You believe all that!' he said wildly – 'But you are wrong – quite wrong! It isn't true – it's all silly superstition! There is no God – no heaven! – there are no such creatures as angels! Oh, you poor, poor man! – you do not know – you have never learnt! There is nothing more for us after death – nothing! – you will never see little Jessamine again – never – never!' He rose slowly from his kneeling position on the turf, looking so old, and weird, and desperate, that Reuben recoiled from him as from something unnatural and monstrous. 'You will put her down there' – he went on – 'in her coffin, with all the jessamine flowers about her, and you will shovel the earth over her, and very soon the worms will crawl over her poor little face, and in and out her curls, and make of her what you would not look at – what you would not *touch*!' – and he trembled violently as with an ague fit – 'And yet you loved her! And you can talk of a God! Why, a God who would wilfully take Jessamine away from you, would be the cruellest, wickedest monster imaginable! What reason could he give – what object could there be, in first giving her to you, and then killing her and making you miserable? No, no! – there is no God; you have not read – you have not studied things, and you do not know – but you are all wrong! There is no God – there is only the Atom which does not care!'

Reuben, filled with alarm as well as grief, thought the boy raved, and endeavoured to take him again into his arms, but Lionel shrank back, and sudderingly repulsed him.

'Poor little fellow, he's just crazed wi' the shock, an' doesn't for the moment know wot he's sayin',' thought the simple-hearted man, as he compassionately watched the childish figure of despair, frozen, as it seemed, into a statuesque immobility on the edge of Jessamine's grave – 'If he could onny cry a bit, 'twould do him good, surely.' And struck by a sudden idea, he said aloud – 'Will ye come wi' me, my dear, an' see Jessamine now, as she lies asleep among her dowers? – 'twouldn't frighten ye – she's just a little smilin' angel, wi' God's love written on her face. Will ye come?'

'No!' answered Lionel loudly, and almost fiercely – 'I cannot! You forget – I came out this morning to see her alive – with all her curls dancing about, and her eyes shining – oh, I was so happy! And all the time she was dead! No, I couldn't look at her – I couldn't! – I should be thinking of this grave . . . and the worms . . . there is one down there just now . . . crawling – crawling – see!' and he suddenly began to laugh deliriously, dry sobs intermingling with his laughter – 'Oh! – and you – you can actually believe it is a good God that has killed Jessamine!'

Flinging his hands up above his head, he suddenly turned away and ran – ran furiously, out of the churchyard, and away up the road, not in the direction of his home, but up towards the deep green woods that hang like a glorious pavilion over the nestling village, giving it shade even in the most scorching heats of the summer sun. Reuben looked after him, wondering and half-afraid.

'God help the child!' he murmured – 'He seems gone clean mad like, in 's grief! An' it's something more than my Jess'-mine's death that's working in 's mind, poor lad – it's a trouble out o' reach somewhere. An' now I mind me he's lost his mother by a far worse partin' than death – disgrace! Ah, well!' and taking up his spade he went resolutely to the resumption of his sad task, carefully smoothing and patting the earth round the interior of his little child's grave with his own tender hands, and removing the poor worm Lionel had perceived, gently and without loathing, in the manner of one for whom all God's creation, even the lowest portion of it, had a certain sacredness because of the Divine Spirit moving in all and through all. 'It's hard for a grown man like me to bear a sorrow – an' it's double hard for a little lad like him. He sees nowt o' God in 'is trouble – onny the trouble itself. Lord help us all for the poor sinful creatures that we be! Ah, Jess'mine, Jess'mine! – my little lass – my little flower! – who'd ha' thought God would ha' wanted ye s'soon!'

Tears rushed to his eyes and blotted out the landscape, falling one by one into the small grave, as he dug it deeper – 'But He's a God o' Love, an' He winnut mind my grievin' a bit – He knows it's just human-like, an' comes from the poor broken heart o' me that's weak an' ignorant – an' by-an'-by, when my mind clears, He'll gi' me grace to see 'twas for the best – aye, for the best! Mother an' child in heaven, an' I alone on earth – all the joy for them, an' all the sorrow for me! – well, that's right enough – an' surely God'll send down both my angels to fetch me when my time comes to go. An' that's onny a little while to wait, my Jess'mine flower! – onny a little while!'

He dashed away his tears, with one hand, and continued digging patiently, till his melancholy work was done – then, untying a bundle of sweet myrtle he had beside him, he completely lined the little grave with the fragrant sprays, making it look like a nest of tender green – and placing two boards above it to protect it from the night-dews and the chance of rain, he shouldered his spade and went slowly homeward, pondering sadly on the heavy trial awaiting him next day, when all that was mortal of his daring child would be committed, with prayer! and holy blessing, to the dust.

Meanwhile, Lionel had passed a strange time of torture alone in the woods. When he ran away from the churchyard he was hardly conscious of what he was doing – and it was not till he found himself in a bosky grove, among thickly planted oaks and pine-trees, that he became aware of his own sentient existence once more. There was a heavy burning pain in his head, and his eyes were aching and dim. He flung himself down on the mossy turf and tried to think. Jessamine was dead! The little laughing thing with the divine blue eyes and the sweet baby smile was lying cold and stiff in her coffin. It seemed incredible! He remembered her as he had last seen her, peeping through the tangle of her own namesake flowers, and saying in her pretty, soft plaintive voice 'Poor Lylie! I'se 'fraid you won't see me never no more!' And then that final farewell – 'Good-bye, Lylie! Not for long!'

Not for long! – and now – it was good-bye for ever! A faint cry broke from the boy's lips – 'Oh, little Jessamine! Poor little Jessamine!' But no tears fell – the fountain of those drops of healing seemed dried up beneath the scorching weight that pressed upon his brain. Jessamine! – could it be possible that there was nothing left of her – nothing but senseless clay? All that trustful tenderness, that lovely innocence, that quaint and solemn faith of hers in Christ, and in the angels – what was it all for? Why should such a sweet and delicate little spirit be created only to perish?

'It is cruel!' he said aloud, turning his pale, small, agonised face up to the network of leafy branches crossing the blue of the sky – 'It is cruel to have made *her* – it is cruel to have made *me* – if death is the only end. It is senseless – even wicked! If death were not all, then I could understand.' He paused, and his eyes rested on a tuft of meadow-sweet growing close beside him – 'Where do you go to when you die?' he asked, addressing the flower – 'Have you what some people call a soul – a soul that takes wings and flies away, to bloom again in a more beautiful shape elsewhere? You might do this – of course you might – and *we* should never know!'

He rose to his feet and stood, musing darkly, with small hands clenched and lips set hard. 'Perhaps the learned men are not so wise as they think – it – it is possible they may be mistaken. The Atom they argue about, may be a God after all – and even Christ who some say is a myth, and others describe as merely a good man who wished to reform the

Jews, may be the Divine Being the Testament tells us of. And there may be another life after this one, and another world, where Jessamine is now. The question is, how to be quite, quite sure of it?' He walked one or two paces – then a sudden though flashed across him – a thought which lit his eyes with strange brilliancy and flushed his cheeks to a feverish red. 'I know!' he whispered, 'I know the best way to discover the real secret – I *must* find it out! – and I will!'

And all at once invested with a curious tranquillity of movement and demeanour, he went slowly out of the woods, and down the hill up which he had scrambled in such frenzied haste – and looking at the ground steadfastly as he walked, he passed the church and churchyard gate, without once raising his eyes. In a few minutes he had entered his father's domain, where he met Professor Cadman-Gore marching briskly up and down the carriage-drive.

'Hullo!' said that gentleman – 'Had a good scramble?'

Lionel made no answer.

The Professor eyed him narrowly.

'Feeling ill again?' he demanded.

Lionel forced a pale smile.

'Not exactly ill' – he answered – 'I've been to the church-yard – and – and the sexton there is digging a grave for his little girl – his only child, who died suddenly of diphtheria while we were away at Clovelly. She was quite a baby – only six – and – and I knew her – her name was Jessamine.'

Professor Cadman-Gore was a little bewildered. The dull precise manner in which the boy spoke – the way he kept his eyes fixed on the ground, and the odd frowning contraction of his brows, struck the worthy preceptor as somewhat singular. But being quite in the dark as to the Jessamine Dale episode, he took refuge in generalities.

'You shouldn't wander about in churchyards' – he said testily – 'Nasty, damp places . . .'

'Yes – where we must all go at last' – said Lionel, still smiling his stiff difficult little smile – 'Down among the worms – all of us – and nothing more!'

'Dear, dear me!' growled the Professor, beginning to feel almost angry – 'I wish you wouldn't talk such nonsense, Lionel – I've told you of it before – it's absolutely provoking!'

'Why?' asked the boy – 'We do die – all of us – don't we?'

'Of course we do – but we needn't talk about it or think about it' – snapped out the Professor – 'While we live, let us live – that was a favourite maxim with the ancient Greeks, who enjoyed both life and learning – and it's a very sensible one too.'

'Do you really think so? – really?' and Lionel looked at him with such an aged and worn puckering of his features that his tutor was quite startled – 'But they were only fools after all – they died – and their cities and wonderful colleges perished – and what was the good of all their learning?'

'It has come down to us!' replied the Professor, drawing himself up, and expanding his meagre chest in a sudden glow of intellectual pride – 'It has formed the foundation of all literature. Isn't that something?'

Lionel sighed: 'I suppose it is – it all depends on how you look at it,' – he said – 'But you see one would like to know where even such a thing as Literature leads to – and where it is to end. I don't think we can trace its actual beginning, because there have been so many civilisations which are all forgotten and buried now. For instance, the ancient Mexicans believed that the existence of the world was made up of five successive ages, and five successive suns – there have been four suns lit and burnt out, according to them, and ours now shining is the fifth – and last! Of course that was only their myth and idea – but I do think everything ever discovered is in time forgotten, and has to begin all over again. It seems very stupid and useless to me – the constant repetition of everything for nothing!'

The Professor glowered severely at him.

'I think you're tired' – he said with affected gruffness – 'You'd better go and sit quietly in the schoolroom, or lie down. It's no use over-fatiguing yourself. And what you wanted to go to the churchyard and see a grave dug for, I can't imagine. It's rather a morbid taste!'

'I didn't go to see a grave dug' – answered Lionel steadily – 'I went to see the little girl – who is dead. I thought she was still alive – I didn't know – I didn't expect . . .' There was a painful throbbing in his throat – he bit his lips hard – anon he resumed slowly – 'You know – for I've often told you – that I can't see any sensible reason why there should be life, or death. Everything seems explainable but that. I am very interested in it – but even you can't tell me what I want to know – and so I must try to find it out as well as I can – by myself.'

He lifted his cap with the usual gentle salute he always gave his tutor, and went indoors. The Professor looked after him with an uncomfortable sense of foreboding.

'An odd boy!' he mused – 'A very odd boy – yet a thinking boy, and clever and docile. If his strength will only hold out he will be a brilliant man and a magnificent scholar – but his health is capricious.' He walked with long strides a few paces, and suddenly stopped, a grim smile playing across his features. 'It's a singular thing – a very singular thing – I should never have thought it possible – but I certainly find him a lovable boy. Positively lovable! It is ridiculous, quite ridiculous of course, that I should find him so – but I do! Yes – positively lovable!'

And he laughed; – his laugh never by any means added to the beauty of his appearance, but on this occasion there was an affectionate twinkle in his filmy eye which might almost be called handsome.

CHAPTER 14

NIGHT came, calm and dewy. There was no moon – and in the depths of the purple ether the great stars ruled supreme. Jupiter rose in all his full effulgence, a golden-helmeted leader among the planet-gods of the sky, and over the unruffled breast of the dark sea Venus hung low like a pendent jewel. Afar off, the outline of the landscape was blurred and indistinct, softening into a fine haze that presented the delicate suggestion of some possible fairyland hidden behind the last dim range of the wood-crowned hills. Through the still air floated a wandering scent of newly-stacked hay and crushed sweet-briar, an almost imperceptible touch of autumn sobered the heavy green foliage of the trees to a deeper sombreness of hue – while over all things reigned a curious and impressive silence, as though the million whispering tongues of Nature had suddenly been checked by the command of that greater Voice which in olden time had hushed the storm with its calm 'Peace! Be still!' In the 'big house' – for so the residence temporarily occupied by Mr. Valliscourt was styled by the villagers of Combmartin – there was an equally solemn silence. Every one was asleep – save Lionel. He, broad awake, sat on the edge of his little bed, with bright eyes a-stare, and brain busily at work, and every pulse and nerve in his body thrilling with excitement. Never had he looked so young as now – a flush of colour was in his cheeks and lips, and the little smile that played across his features from time to time, was, if somewhat vague, still singularly sweet and expressive of pleasure. He had gone to bed at the usual hour – he had said 'Good-night' to his father, who had been reading the evening paper, and who had merely looked over the edge of it and nodded by way of response – he had then gone to Professor Cadman-Gore who was poring over an enormous quarto volume printed in black-letter, and who answered absently – 'Good-night? Yes – er – ah! Of course! Certainly – very good indeed! You are going to bed – exactly! – that's right!' and so murmuring, had pressed his little hand kindly, and then had resumed his book-worm burrowings. And he had called dowstairs to housemaid Lucy, 'Good-night!' a thing he rarely ever did; and she had replied from the kitchen depths, 'Good-night, Master Lionel!' in a bright tone of surprise and pleasure agreeable to hear. And then he had reached his bedroom – but he had not undressed, or prepared for bed at all, or laid his head down on the pillow for a moment. Clad in the navy-blue jersey suit he had worn all day, he only slipped off his shoes in order not to make any noise, and then he paced softly up and down his room thinking, thinking all the while. Such a whirl of thoughts too! Thick as snowflakes, and as dizzying to the brain, thoughts seemed to rain upon him, fire-red and flame-white – for they took strange burning colours, and ran in strange grooves. He had put out his candle – he liked the sensation of moving to and fro in the darkness, as then he could imagine things. For instance he could imagine his mother was with him, sitting just in the very chair where she had sat when she rocked him in her arms and called him her 'baby' – and so strong was the delusion he excited in himself that he actually went and knelt down beside her visionary figure and said,

'Mother! Mother darling, I love you! I shall always love you!' and then had laughed a little and shuddered, as he realised that after all it was only his fancy – that she was gone – gone for ever! – and that he was quite alone.

And presently, retreating to the window, and looking out into the starlit night, he thought he could see Jessamine standing in the garden below, with a wreath of her flowers round her hair, and her blue eyes upturned to him where he watched her – yes! he could even hear her calling:

'Lylie! Lylie! Come an' play!' And he almost felt inclined

to open the window and jump down to that little shadow-figure on the dark turf – till he suddenly bethought him that it was a mistake – Jessamine was dead – her grave was ready – she was going to be put down into the earth and hidden away from the sunshine – she would never call him any more – never! Hurrying away from the corner whence he could see her so plainly, and where it frightened him to look out at her lonely little ghost in the garden, he climbed up on his bed and sat there, swaying his feet to and fro, and thinking – still thinking. He heard his father come up the stairs with a firm and heavy tread, enter his bedroom, and shut and lock the door – then the Professor followed, coughing loudly and shuffling his slippered feet along the landing to the apartment he occupied at the very end of the corridor – and presently the old ‘ grandfather's clock’ in the hall below, chimed eleven. After this the great silence fell – the silence that was so mystically suggestive of undiscoverable things.

And Lionel listened as it were, to that silence, till he grew restless under its spell. Springing off his bed, he lit his candle in haste, and looked nervously round him as though he half expected to see some one in the room – then, rallying his forces, he softly opened a large cupboard that was made to appear like a part of the wall, and setting a chair within it, stood thereon, and reached his hand up to the corner of a particular shelf, where, snugly secreted in the pocket of one of his little overcoats, he kept the ‘baby-sash’ his mother had given him as a parting souvenir. Taking possession of this, he got down from the chair, put it back in its place, and shut the cupboard carefully again – then he stood still for a moment, thinking. After a little while, he unfolded and shook out the sash to its full length, and dreamily admired its pretty blue colour and the graceful design of the daisy-chain so deftly woven upon it. Re-folding it once more, he slipped it inside his vest – then putting on his shoes by mere force of habit, he took his candlestick – the candle in it burning steadily –

and opening his bedroom door listened breathlessly. There was not a sound in the house – not so much as a crack of wood in the old Chippendale press that stood up, gaunt and shadowy on the outer landing. Swiftly and noiselessly, holding the light well above his head that he might see clearly and not stumble, he sped downstairs to the school-room. The door was wide open, and as he went in and pushed it to after him, he gave a sigh of relief and satisfaction, as though he had attained at last some long-desired goal of ambition.

There was more light in this apartment than in his bedroom; there were no trees to shadow the window and through its crossed lattice-panes the stars twinkled with a white brilliance not unworthy of the moon herself. Setting his candle on the table-desk at which he had worked so many weary hours and days pondering on things that never would, and never could be of any use to anyone's practical afterlife, Lionel took out paper, pen and ink, and seating himself, proceeded to write certain words with careful slowness and most business-like precision. Shaping his letters roundly and neatly, he took a great deal of pains to make his meaning unmistakably clear, and having covered one sheet of paper, he folded it in four with mathematical exactitude, addressed it and commenced another. When this was also done, he folded it in the same way as the first, and addressed it likewise – then he put the two missives together on the table, one beside the other, and looked at them with a kind of naive interest and admiration. Their superscriptions were turned uppermost, and one read thus

'*To my Father.*
John Valliscourt Esq. Of Valliscourt.'

The other was more simply inscribed –

'*To Professor Cadman-Gore.*'

For some minutes he studied these addresses minutely and with something of a smile on his face.

'It is just as if I were going to run away!' he said half aloud, 'And so I am! That is exactly what I am going to do. I am going to run away!' And the smile deepened. 'I remember what Willie Montrose told me – "rather than break down altogether you'd better show a clean pair of heels." And that's just what I'm going to do. By the bye, I never sent poor Willie his Homer.'

He rose, and turning towards the book-shelves, two of which were ranged along the opposite wall, soon found the volume and packed it neatly up in readiness for posting, addressing it in a large clear hand to 'W. Montrose, Esq., B.A., The Nest, Kilmun, Scotland.' Then after considering awhile, he sat down again and wrote another letter, which ran as follows –

DEAR WILLIE,

You left your favourite copy of Homer behind when you said good-bye to me. I meant to have sent it to you before, but somehow it slipped my memory. Now, as I am going away, it might get mislaid among my father's books, so I have left it with Professor Cadman-Gore (who is a very nice old man) all ready for him to post to you. Thank you for all your kindness to me – I have never forgotten it, and I'm almost sure I shall never forget. You needn't be anxious about me any more – I'm all right.

Your affectionate and grateful
LIONEL.

He put this letter in an envelope which he addressed, but left open, and wrote a slip of paper which he laid above it and the Homer volume together, giving the following instruction:

DEAR PROFESSOR – Will you please post this letter and also the book, to Mr. Montrose for me. It is his copy of Homer which he left with me by mistake, and he is sure to want it.

LIONEL.

'That's done!' he said, as he wiped his pen and put by the ink and paper in their respective places with his usual methodical neatness – 'It's no use writing to mother – if I did, she would never get the letter.'

He went to the window, and opened it. It was a glorious night – and as he threw back the lattice, the sweet air flowed in, laden with a thousand delicious odours from the forest and ocean. So deep was the stillness that he could barely hear the vague murmur of small waves lapping the shore now and again, though the sea was not half a mile distant. It was such a night as when the trustful and believing heart is filled like a holy chalice with the rich wine of joy and gratitude – when the soul rises to an angel's stature within its fleshy tenement, and sings 'Magnificat!' – when Nature wears her most serene and noble aspect – when it seems good to live, good to work, good to hope, good to love – good to be even the smallest portion of the divine and splendid order of the Universe. But to the young boy who stood gazing out on the infinite majesty of the moving earth and heavens, there was no order, but mere chaos – a black conflicting contradiction of forces – a non-reasoning production of things that neither sought nor desired existence, and that have no sooner learned to love life than they are plunged into death and eternal nothingness. In the 'Free-Thinker's Catechism' (Catechisme du Libre-Penseur), by one Edgar Monteil – a code of ethics which has been circulated assiduously among children's schools in France for some years – the unhappy little beings whose ideas of morality are engrafted upon this atheistical doctrine, are taught that 'the passions of man are his surest and most faithful guides,' and that 'God is a spectre invented by priests to frighten timid minds;' – this, too, in utter and wicked oblivion of the grand truth proclaimed with such a grand simplicity – 'God is love!' 'As the soul,' writes the self-deluded compiler of the 'Free-Thinker's Catechism,' 'no longer constitutes for us an independent and imperishable individuality, there is no future life.' And what are the results of this 'new' confession of faith? Too terrible and devastating to be easily gauged, though something of their danger may be gathered from the discussions of the *Conseil d'Arrondissement de Nantes*, the members of which declare that – 'Considering that the suicides of young children and persons of tender age (formerly almost unknown among us) have multiplied recently to such a degree as to reach the alarming extent of 443 cases in one year' – and furthermore 'considering the deplorable increase of vice and crime among children and youths we take the vow – says the council with almost passionate solemnity – 'that in the schools of this *Arrondissement*, morality shall not be separated from religion, and that the teaching of duty towards GOD shall be the fundamental and necessary base of all duties which are incumbent upon man.'

Such is the wise decision of Nantes – but unhappily the good example is not followed throughout France in general. In almost every educational department the principles of the 'Libre-Penseur' are sowing the seeds of ruin to the nation, and making of the average human being a creature worse than the lowest and most untamable of ferocious beasts. And these principles, largely adopted by the Free-Thinking societies in England, are being gradually disseminated among the children of our own secular schools – for the agents or 'missionaries' of Free-Thought are to the full as active in distributing their tracts and pamphlets as the most fervid Salvationist that ever tossed the 'War-Cry' in the faces of the public; – more stealthy in their movements, they are none the less cunning; and in our once God-fearing country, many can now be found who passively accept as truth the deadening and blasphemous lie uttered in the words – 'As the soul no longer constitutes an independent and imperishable individuality, there is no future life!'

And yet, in sober earnest this 'independent and imperishable individuality' is more self assertive than ever it was – it passionately claims to be heard and acknowledged – it clamours with all its immortal strength at the barriers of the Unknown, crying, 'Open! – Open! Unveil the hidden Glory which *I* know and feel, yet cannot speak of! Open! – that Doubt may see, and seeing, die!' For the Soul in each one of us is instinctively aware that the hidden Glory exists – though it cannot explain in mortal speech why, whence, or how. Nevertheless the Psyche feels her lover; and through the darkness of earth's perplexities stretches out yearning hands to grasp the actual Divine which Is, and which reveals itself to mortals in a thousand subtle tender ways of promise, warning, knowledge or sweet comfort. But our lamps of learning, ill-trimmed and dull, cannot shed light on such Eternal Splendour – they needs must be extinguished in the greater radiance, even as sparks in a blaze of sunshine.

Little Lionel, dimly conscious of 'the imperishable and independent individuality' in his own slight frame, though he could not analyse what he felt, gazed straight out on the shining planets, which, like great golden eyes, regarded him as straightly, and thought what a strange thing it was that there should be millions and millions of worlds in the sky, all created by an Atom, for Nothing! If he had been a man, grown callous and cold-hearted through the sameness of life as generally lived, he might possibly have found with Edgar Monteil, some satisfaction in the terrific satire – 'The passions of man are his surest and most faithful guides,' – but being only a child, he had no passions save an endless desire to know – a desire that nothing ever written by all the atheists in the world will satisfy or restrain. A child's first inquiries concerning spiritual and transcendent things, need noble answers envolved from purest thought – for, as the Italian proverb has it – 'The "why" of a child is the key of philosophy.' Woe betide those who crush the high aspirations of innocent and hopeful youth by the deadening blow of Materialism! Worse than murderers are they, and as a greater crime than murder shall they answer for it! For truly has it been said – 'Fear not them which kill the body, but fear them which kill the soul.' Killing the soul is the favourite occupation of the so-called 'wise men' of today; – spreading their pernicious influence through the Press, and through current literature, they congratulate themselves when they have dragged their readers down into a slough of pessimism and atheism, and caused them to think of God as the supreme Evil, instead of the supreme Good. Yet every anti-Christian author nowadays has his or her commendatory clique, and salvo of applause from the Press, and the more blasphemous, vulgar and obscene the work, the louder the huzzas. In this way, things are tending fast towards the attitude of the 'Libre-Penseur,' so that soon when the children ask us 'Who made heaven and earth?' we shall answer flippantly according to that Catechism – 'Neither the heaven, nor infinity, nor the earth has been created.'

Question. 'There is no First Cause then?'

Answer. 'No – for all that we cannot prove scientifically has no existence.'

And here was the boy Lionel's difficulty. He was actively conscious of something he could not 'prove scientifically,' and it was impossible for him to believe that that something 'had no existence.' For IT – that undefinable vague Something – to him meant Everything. As he stood at the open window looking at the stars, the impression of a sudden vastness, an all-sufficing Goodness and Perfection, swept over his mind, like a wave rolling in upon him from the Infinite, giving him a vague yet soothing sense of peace.

'It is beautiful!' he murmured – 'Beautiful to think that in a very little while I shall know all – why, I may even meet Jessamine the very first thing – who can tell! It is wrong, I daresay, to want to find out so quickly – but I couldn't bear to go on and on every day, learning a lot of useless things, and always missing the one thing.'

The Dennis Wheatley Library of the Occult

In this paperback series we propose to include novels and uncanny tales by:

Marjorie Bowen, John Buchan, Ambrose Bierce, R. H. and E. F. Benson, Brodie-Innes, Balzac, Algernon Blackwood, F. Marion Crawford, Wilkie Collins, Aleister Crowley, Dickens, Conan Doyle, Dostoyevsky, Lord Dunsany, Guy Endore, Dion Fortune, Kipling, Le Fanu, Bulwer Lytton, Walter de la Mare, A. E. W. Mason, Arthur Machen, John Masefield, Guy de Maupassant, Oliver Onions, Edgar Allan Poe, Sax Rohmer, Bram Stoker, W. B. Seabrook, H. G. Wells, Hugh Walpole and Oscar Wilde.

Also books on:
Palmistry, Astrology, Faith healing, Clairvoyance, Numerology, Telepathy, etc.

For particulars write to Sphere Books Ltd., 30/32 Gray's Inn Road, London WC1X 8JL.

All Sphere Books are available at your bookshop or newsagent, or can be ordered from the following address: Sphere Books, Cash Sales Department, P.O. Box 11, Falmouth, Cornwall.

Please send cheque or postal order (no currency), and allow 7p per copy to cover the cost of postage and packing in U.K. or overseas.

Black Magic titles by Dennis Wheatley
published by Arrow Books

THE DEVIL RIDES OUT

GATEWAY TO HELL

THE HAUNTING OF TOBY JUGG

THE KA OF GIFFORD HILLARY

THE SATANIST

STRANGE CONFLICT

THEY USED DARK FORCES

TO THE DEVIL – A DAUGHTER

A serious study of the Occult, fully illustrated
THE DEVIL AND ALL HIS WORKS

If you would like a complete list of Arrow Books, including
other Dennis Wheatley titles, please send a postcard to
P.O. Box 29, Douglas, Isle of Man, Great Britain.